The Sapphire Ring
is the third book in
A Leslie LaRue Mystery Series
by Molly Owen

More books in
A Leslie LaRue Mystery Series
from Molly Owen

First
The Lost Medallion
Second
The Antique Clock

*Please see back of the book for a preview
of the next Christian Romance, filled with
mystery, emotion, and surprise.*

by Molly Owen
The Red Lady Inn

The Sapphire Ring

A LESLIE LARUE MYSTERY

Molly Owen

I dedicate this book to my father, the gentlest man I ever knew, full of strength, courage, and faith.

ACKNOWLEDGMENTS

Many times while writing, I found the direction of the story takes on a life of its own. This was one of those times. Whether influence from events in my own life or just tuning in to the path the story should take I found myself intrigued with the results. Extreme emotions are presented as a question of our own reactions to crisis and our faith in God's presence in our lives. So this, the third book in the Leslie LaRue series, following *The Lost Medallion* and *The Antique Clock,* took a little longer than expected.

Anyone who has visited or lived in the French Quarter can not escape feeling the soul of this place, filled with longing and hope. This Nola is a safe place to be who we are, to find ourselves, and discover our innate talent. As we continue with the same characters living in New Orleans we share the traditions, the culture, and lifestyle of this unique place that leads us to mysteries and struggles we all find ourselves in at one time or another.

The positive feedback from my wonderful friends and faithful family who have pushed for the completion of this book kept me on course. I want to thank them for their patience while acknowledging their desire to read the next book in the series. I am blessed by the Christian fellowship from my friends and their positive response to my efforts to entertain while giving them food for thought.

A special thank you goes to my daughter, Janie, who once again created the beautiful cover of this book. Her expertize in book publishing has helped me become a better author with each effort while allowing me to create this series.

PROLOGUE

The long-awaited construction had begun on the studio behind their home and Leslie LaRue Rye, an author, looked forward to a private place to write. Her husband, Sidney Rye, was busy with Rye Detective Services leaving her to deal with the contractors while writing her latest book and keeping track of their four-year-old, Ryan. Daisy the Nanny did an excellent job of caring for him. Leslie just had a hard time not interacting with her son.

Leslie, Sidney, and their friend Annabelle Robicheaux, the lawyer, had spent the last several months on a case involving embezzlement of family trust funds. The trial over, they were breathing a sigh of relief. Leslie, like Sidney and Annabelle, was a very effective investigator. Her help on the Jonathon Bordeaux case had been invaluable even though putting Leslie in danger.

Two positive things were a direct result of the trial. Jonathon committed his life to Christ while in jail and was exhibiting to others the peace and tranquility he derived from his relationship with God. Annabelle and Jeffrey, Jonathon's younger brother, fell in love while working together on a better understanding of the charges against Jonathon. They were spending more time together now that it wouldn't put Annabelle in jeopardy of conflict of interest while representing Jonathon. Very much in love, they were getting to know each other out in the open rather than in secret.

The Bordeaux family was putting the pieces back together as they faced their own feelings about Jonathon and the family trust. The siblings in order, Jonathon, Rose Marie (and her husband, Patrick), Robert (and his wife, Sandy), Jeffrey, Katrina Louise, and A.J., the baby sister, were heirs to the family trust. However, the assets were now gone.

Chapter **1**

Opening the gate attached to the cornstalk fence, she carefully walked through the unkempt lawn overgrown by months of neglect. Her high heels sank as she looked for the path leading to the front porch, or in New Orleans called the galley, behind large round pillars. Putting the key in the familiar lock on the Greek door she turned it and pushed the door open revealing the massive spiral staircase. She always imagined, as a child, she would walk down those very stairs in her wedding gown to meet her prince charming.

She stood in awe remembering years past spent in her childhood home. Everything looked the same, but the heart of the home was gone. Tears came to her eyes and the lump in her throat made it hard to swallow. Shaking her head to clear her mind, she went to the kitchen. Her mother's cooking utensils were still in the same container on the stove, and the big stirring spoon in the ceramic holder waited for the next stir. It was as if her mother had just left the room. She found herself putting things away in their proper place, wiping down the dusty counter, closing the drawers and cabinet doors. She then took the broom from the pantry and began to sweep the floor gathering dust and debris in a pile, and scooping it into a dustpan.

"There. That's better," she said to the empty room.

Katrina Louise had a good income as a real-estate broker, selling and flipping houses, but this was different. It was never her intention to own this house that sat outside the French Quarter in New Orleans. This Greek Revival Style house designed by James Gallier Sr. the architect of many homes in the Garden District, was her family's home, and when the bank put it on the market for a Quick Sale her heart spoke to her and, she made the decision based on emotion. However, she knew this decision would put her in trouble with her siblings. Her older brother, Jeffrey, closest to her in birth order, was her go-to person when she felt stumped. Unable to think straight, she pushed his number in her speed dial and waited for him to answer.

"Hi Sis, how have you been, haven't heard from you lately?" Jeffrey said leaning back in his chair away from his desk.

"I've been good, I guess, but when I tell you what I've done, you may not think I'm in my right mind."

"The verdict has always been out on that, Sis. So, what have you done now?"

"Well, when the bank put the folk's home up for a quick sale, I let my emotions get the best of me and well, Jeffrey, I bought it," she said waiting for the condemnation from her sibling.

"Really?" Jeffrey said surprised by his sister's usual sane decisions.

"So, what do you think? Am I crazy?"

"I'll have to give this one some thought," Jeffrey replied leaning forward, putting the legs of the chair back on the floor. He pulled his broad shoulders in toward his chest in a protective mode stretching his back and shoulders trying to release the stress he was feeling. Then taking a deep breath lifted his head and removed his glasses putting them down on the desk. *I really thought we were through with all of this and could move on.* He thought.

"I don't know what I was thinking. I don't want to live in this big ole house. I like living in the French Quarter where all the action is. You know what I mean? I guess I thought I could turn it like the others I've done in the Garden District, but Jeffrey I'll really feel guilty if it turns a good profit. What will the other's think?"

In answer to his silence, she continued. "I choked up when I came inside, so many memories hung in the air like a ghost. I put the kitchen back in order with all of mom's things in their place, and the whole time I felt like she was right there showing me where everything went. I'm amazed that most things are just like she left it. Upstairs, the beds are still made, the chest of drawers and closets are full. It's just so eerie," she said, sitting at the bottom of the staircase.

"That is strange, I mean about everything untouched. I don't know. I would've thought Jonathon would've been in the house. But then maybe the bank took it over and changed the locks so he couldn't get in," Jeffrey contemplated.

"My thought exactly. Maybe he felt guilty. Who knows what was going on in his head?" Katrina Louise said, standing up and walking to the parlor.

"You might ask everyone if they want anything in the house even though I'm surprised that the bank didn't have a sale or something to recoup their losses," Jeffrey said trying to wrap his head around what this meant going forward. "By the way, not to change the subject, I have some news. I've asked Annabelle to marry me."

"Oh Jeffrey, that's wonderful. You two are meant for each other. When is the wedding?"

"We haven't set a date, working out some logistics, soon I hope. I haven't given her a ring yet. I want it to be special."

"She's so fortunate to have you, Jeffrey. You'll make a wonderful husband."

"Thank you, Sis, now back to your dilemma, if you want, I can help you with the place, you know sorting through things,"

"Oh, would you Jeffrey, that would be great. I'll give you a call later, and set up the day and time. I love you, big brother," she said relieved. "And just a little side note, it didn't bother me to see remnants of my one and only marriage. I walked down the staircase exactly like I dreamt it would be and the reception in the garden was perfect. The only thing missing was a lasting marriage with lots of love. I guess that is why it doesn't bother me," she said trying to convince herself.

Taking a deep cleansing breath, Jeffrey set his cell phone on the desk while collecting his thoughts. In his heart, he knew everything didn't end at the conclusion of the trial, however, the stress his family had endured for those months before Jonathon went on trial were almost unbearable. To deal with the siblings again on the issue of the house was not something he was looking forward to under the best of circumstances.

His brother Jonathon, the oldest of six children, had gone on trial for embezzling funds from the family trust. As anyone could imagine, the whole ordeal pit brothers and sisters against each other. Now his sister the realtor had managed to open the wound by buying the house that was in the trust. Just the thought of what this could stir up in the family made his head hurt and coming at a time when he and Annabelle were ready to start a new chapter in their life made matters worse. He wasn't prepared to take this on with his sister and was having second thoughts about volunteering to help her with the house.

He and Katrina Louise had always been close, even after both finished college they stayed involved in each other's lives. A couple of years older he felt a responsibility for her. He was there for her after her failed marriage and helped her get her footing in the real-estate business when she sold him her first listing, a shotgun house perfect for the most handsome eligible bachelor in town.

Katrina Louise knew she could count on her brother in a pinch and sure enough, he came through. She walked around the stately home making a list of the things that would need to be taken care of, either repaired or cleaned. Basically, the place was in good shape, needing more cosmetic than anything. The grounds required attention, and the cornstalk iron fences would need repair and possibly new paint. Carpet would need to be taken up to expose the original floors. Chandeliers would need to be cleaned and drapes taken to the cleaners. All and all it was more elbow grease than money to put it back on the historic register.

*****

"Hi Annabelle, I know you're busy, just wanted to invite you and Jeffrey to dinner tonight if you don't have other plans. Sidney and I haven't seen much of you two since the trial, and we thought a quiet dinner with just the four of us would really be nice."

"Oh Leslie that sounds great, let me check with Jeffrey and get back with you, and Leslie I have something to tell you that you won't believe," Annabelle said.

"No, not another mystery. One of your clients perhaps?" Leslie said teasing her friend, Annabelle, the attorney.

"Jeffrey just called before you did, and told me his sister, Katrina Louise actually bought their folk's house. You know the one the bank was going to foreclose on because the second mortgage was due and the trust was unable to pay it off."

"What on earth was she thinking?" Leslie said exasperatedly.

"I know. Jeffrey is stunned, and somehow she got him to offer to help with sorting things out. The siblings in that family always stick up for each other, and Jeffrey felt sorry for her, even though it was her decision. He said she told him it was an emotional decision because of the memories of growing up in the house."

"Unbelievable," Leslie said.

"I know. I'll call you back as soon as I check with Jeffrey about dinner."

Leslie, the writer, mulled over in her head the information Annabelle had just told her. In the middle of writing her next book, she briefly contemplated weaving in a new story line based on this family. However, the book was moving along in spite of the noise from the construction of the studio going on behind their house. Grateful that when it is done she would have space to write in private, she decided to save the Bordeaux family antics for another book.

She had a feeling there was more on Annabelle's mind that she was letting on. *Is it because of Jeffrey's involvement with his folk's house or is it something else.* Neither having siblings, Annabelle and Leslie, as close friends, were more like sisters. They understood each other, and had been through thick and thin together, allowing the feeling to surface when either one was in crisis. Leslie bowed her head in prayer. *Almighty God, to you, be the Glory, thank you for the gift of salvation through your son Jesus Christ. Thank you, for all blessings and for your forgiveness of our sins. Be with Jeffrey and Annabelle facing a new event in their lives. Give them guidance, patience, and forgiving hearts in this situation. I pray this in Jesus' Name. Amen.*

"So what do you think will happen going forward?" Sidney said standing next to Leslie in their kitchen preparing the steaks for the grill. "Do you think Jeffrey will want to talk about it at dinner tonight?"

"If he does, I think we should let him take the lead, and hear him out. I don't know if he knows Annabelle shared that with me."

"Yeah, you're probably right. Everything seems to be on time, potatoes in the oven, a salad made, which—by the way—looks delicious, and steaks ready for the grill. So they should be here anytime now," Sidney said covering the meat with aluminum foil. Virtually on cue, the doorbell rang.

Jeffrey went out to the back of the house with Sidney to put the steaks on the grill. Annabelle followed Leslie to the kitchen as Leslie handed her a glass of red wine. "This is a new wine we are trying. It has gooseberry in it, and it takes some getting used to. What do you think?"

"I'm not sure yet. It must be an acquired taste," Annabelle said, putting the glass back on the counter.

"Here, I have some white wine," Leslie said handing her friend another glass.

It wasn't long until the men came back in with steaks and the four of them set the rest of the food on the table.

Sidney said the blessing, "Thank you, Father, for a beautiful day, and for two of our favorite people sharing this meal with us.

Bless this food for the nourishment of our bodies, and Lord bless this friendship. In His Holy name, Amen."

"Thank you, Sidney," Jeffrey said, and Annabelle nodded in agreement.

After finishing the meal, the four sat around the table enjoying coffee and a slice of the layered Big Chocolate Cake that Annabelle brought from Pat O'Brien's in the French Quarter. The silence was noticeable as they enjoyed bite after bite of the scrumptious dessert when finally, Jeffrey wiped chocolate from his mouth with his napkin and cleared his throat.

Taking Annabelle's hand, he announced their engagement to the delight of Leslie who got up and went around the table and gave Annabelle a tight squeeze and Sidney shook hands with Jeffrey congratulating them both.

"I think this calls for a toast, I'll be right back," Sidney said heading for the kitchen.

Pouring wine in the four stemmed glasses, Sidney put the bottle down and raised his glass to the center of the table. "May all your dreams be fulfilled, and your days bring happiness. And may God always be the center of your commitment to each other."

"Thank you, Sidney, that was beautiful," Annabelle said with tears in her eyes. "We are so blessed to have wonderful friends like the two of you and a good example of the true meaning of marriage."

"I'll drink to that," Jeffrey said raising his glass. The rest of the evening was spent celebrating until everyone remembered their next day would start without them if they didn't get some rest. Jeffrey and Annabelle said their goodbyes, and after shutting and locking the front door, Sidney helped Leslie clear the table.

Dishes put away, Leslie folded her apron and draped the dish towel over the sink while Sidney finished sweeping the kitchen floor.

"I guess Jeffrey had his mind on other things tonight and that's why he didn't bring anything up about the house," Sidney said emptying the dustpan into the trash container.

"They really looked happy, didn't they? I'm so thrilled for Annabelle, she deserves this, and she has found a good man to spend her life with." Leslie said, putting her arms around Sidney's neck. "I found me a good man too," she said looking up at Sidney.

He leaned down and kissed her. "I think I'm the one who found a good woman, Mrs. Rye," he said then taking her hand he led her upstairs.

*****

A week had passed, and Katrina Louise called her contractor, Jean-Paul to come over to give her an estimate on the work that needed to be done on the house. He couldn't take on any more projects because he had more than enough to do but he knew someone who could use the work if she wanted his number.

"Is he reliable?"

"Have him give you some references because I know he has done other work here in New Orleans and that'll give you an idea of the kind of work he does. I wish I could help you, but right now I'm booked for at least six weeks. His name is Nick, Nick Nixson" Jean-Paul told her.

"Okay, give me his number, and I'll give him a call, thank you, Jean Paul, I'm glad you're busy, but I really like working with you so call me when you need work," she said.

After her conversation with Nick, Katrina Louise called his references and set up a time to meet him at the house. Just to be on the safe side since she didn't know him, she asked Jeffrey to be there when she talked to him.

When Jeffrey opened the door in answer to the doorbell, he was face-to-face with a ruddy looking character with a dark beard and sideburns that had not been groomed in a while and black curly shoulder-length hair. His very muscular tattooed arms bulged from the shoulders indicating either he worked out at the gym or was a laborer of sorts. All of this in sharp contrast to Jeffrey's clean shaven, handsome face, well-kept graying hair, dark gray suit and starched shirt with a gold stick pin in the collar holding in his silk tie. About the same height, they stood eye to eye.

"You must be Nick," Jeffrey said offering his hand, then shutting the door behind them. "Katrina Louise is upstairs. She'll be down in a moment."

"So, your wife has taken on quite a project," he said looking around at the stately room with floor to ceiling windows and walls that climbed to the sky with medallions in the ceilings holding nineteenth-century Venetian glass chandeliers that highlight a marble surround on the large fireplace and hearth.

"She's not my wife," Jeffrey said noting the smirk on Nick's face before he could continue. "She's my sister."

"I see, so you must be the money man, every woman needs a project, and this one will take some money," Nick snorted noting the look of wealth on Jeffrey.

"Actually, Katrina Louise is a very astute business person, and I might add, very capable of handling things without my help. This isn't the first house she has renovated or bought, and sold. She's a very successful real estate broker. A word of advice, she doesn't go much for macho men, in fact, if you want her to hire you, you might want to change your attitude about women, if you know what I mean," Jeffrey said, not impressed at all with this so-called male specimen.

Just then, Katrina Louise walked down the stairs toward Nick and Jeffrey. Nick was stunned at her beauty. Jeffrey noticed Nick's reaction to his sister's perfectly coiffured dark hair, business suit with a skirt that struck just above the knee and high heel shoes that accentuated her shapely legs. Carrying a notepad, she approached Nick and offered her hand for a shake. He took her hand and was surprised at the firmness as they shook hands.

"Nick, I presume," she said. "Glad to meet you I'm Katrina Louise Bordeaux, and I see you have met my brother. Let's go into the parlor shall we, and go over some things I'll expect to be done, and get your estimate of not only the labor cost but the estimated time of completion," she said leading them to the round table in the middle of the room.

"My estimate will include material, labor, hiring outside help and time of completion," Nick told her trying to be as businesslike as she presented.

"I'll furnish material to save the cost of your markup, you just tell me what you need, and I'll have it delivered. As far as hiring outside help besides yourself, I'll need to approve of anyone working on the project," she said firmly, looking him straight in the eye. "They will be working for me under your supervision, and I'll hold you responsible for any errors on your part or theirs. We will have a legal contract between us copied and filed with the county. Are there any questions?"

Jeffrey could hardly contain his need to laugh while watching the smirk on Nick's face disappear. *You can't say he wasn't warned.* He said to himself. *This is probably the first time someone has put him in his place*. He was proud of his sister for sizing this character up before doing business with him.

"I checked a couple of your references, which were acceptable by the way. However, each one, without fail, told me you had a hard time letting them control what happened throughout the project. This will not happen with this project. I'll be in charge, and you will follow my direction concerning all points of the project. If you disagree with my perspective, then we'll discuss it. However, you'll not proceed until I agree to the way forward, is that understood?"

"I must admit this is a new way of doing business. I've always had free reign where a decision on the job is made. If you expect me to run everything by you then we may have a problem with the estimated time and cost of labor, due to the delay of the job that infringes on my time. I have no issue with you making the decisions, however, I feel if we understand each other from the beginning there will be no downtime, and we can move forward. I'm an experienced General Contractor, and I expect my clients to take that into consideration when hiring me," Nick said in the calmest voice he could muster.

"I too have had experiences not only with GC's but the people they hire and my experience has taught me to have everything in writing and have constant communication. I'm not a housewife remodeling her kitchen. This is my business, remodeling houses in the Garden District to turn a profit. I know what I want, and I know how it needs to be done. I have many contacts for supplies and experts in all fields from flooring to décor, and I'll rely on them when necessary. If you find this to be daunting, then perhaps we will not be able to work together."

"Let's see what you have in mind first and go from there," Nick said curiously to see what she wanted to be done to the place.

They headed for the kitchen with Jeffrey following close behind not to protect his sister from Nick but to protect Nick from his sister. After a complete tour of the house and gardens, the three went back in the house. Nick told Katrina Louise he would like to work with her on the project and would get back with her on the estimate. After he left Katrina Louise asked Jeffrey what his thoughts were.

"About the house changes, or Nick?"

"Both," she said

"Well, I like the changes in the house. I think we'll need help clearing things out, so the work can be done. As far as Nick is concerned, he seems to know what he's doing if you can work with him. I think both of you are pretty strong willed so if that's not a problem I think he can do the job and do it to your liking, it's almost like a challenge to show you he can do it your way," Jeffrey told her. He had a meeting uptown with some investors and needed to leave so giving his sister a quick kiss on the cheek he said goodbye and wished her luck with her decision about Nick.

*****

That night Jeffrey and Annabelle finished the meal she had prepared, and after they cleared the table he poured them a glass of wine, and they went to the living room. He liked spending time with her in her own space where she was comfortable. Even though she had been to his place in uptown New Orleans, a couple of times, they seemed to gravitate to her home in the French Quarter.

"That was wonderful. I didn't know you were such a good cook. Just one more secret you've kept from me," he said smiling.

"I don't remember keeping secrets from you," Annabelle said a little curious as to what he thought was a secret.

"Well, we could start with how well you play the Harp, then what a great attorney you are, and we must not forget how devoted you are to your detective friends Sidney and Leslie. These were all things I didn't know about you before, and now one by one your talents and desires are coming to the surface," he said sitting next to her on the massive leather sofa.

"I see, so not really secrets just unknowns, things we have discovered about each other. Like the fact you play the piano, you don't cook, but you know where the best restaurants are, and you're devoted to your family. Speaking of which, how did your meeting with Katrina Louise's new contractor go?" she said putting her glass on the table and laying her head on his shoulder.

"This guy, Nick, is quite a character. He looks like he just came off a chain gang," Jeffrey said shaking his head. "I sure wouldn't want to meet him in a dark alley somewhere."

"Really, are you worried about him enough that you don't want him around Katrina Louise?"

"I don't know. I guess I just wish I knew more about him. Sis checked his references as far as his work was concerned but I would be more at ease if I had a background check."

"Why don't you ask Sidney to check him out, you know where he came from, how long he has lived here in the Quarter, if he has any priors, things like that. For that matter, I bet Leslie would be glad to do it for you. She knows how to dig beyond what is on the surface. Her research has helped me more than once in a court case."

"I was thinking about asking you and the Rye's to help me and Katrina Louise clean out the house, so they could start working," he said mulling over what Annabelle had said.

"You know I'll be glad to help, and I think the Rye's would too. So think about asking Leslie to do some research for you when you ask them to help."

Chapter **2**

The Rye Detective Agency was in overload with just two agents. Sidney was working three cases, and his partner was on two more. Sidney was glad for the work, but the late nights away from Leslie and their son, Ryan didn't make for a happy wife. Leslie was having to make decisions about the construction of the Studio behind their home in the Garden District outside of the French Quarter while writing another novel, number eight. Four-year-old Ryan was not only walking and talking at record speed but was asking a million questions a minute. He was missing Sidney, so today the three of them were going on a road trip up the coast.

"Did you get a break in that case you're working on?" Leslie asked.

"Not really, it's not easy to track down jewelry when you don't know where it came from or who bought it. It's like a needle in a haystack. It's obvious this ring of jewelry thieves is operating in the French Market but catching them is another thing. They are far too clever so far," Sidney said a little frustrated.

"You'll get them, just have patience," Leslie said helping carry the things to the beach while Sidney took care of Ryan.

It was a beautiful sunny day, and the water was calm. They laid out their blanket and Leslie gave Ryan his sand buckets. It wasn't long until Ryan and Sidney were building a sand castle while Leslie soaked up some sun. Eyes closed she thought about the book she was working on. She was about midway through and wanted to finish it soon, but for the first time in her writing career, she had hit a dry spell. This had never happened to her as her writing always flowed seamlessly. But now, with Ryan getting older, construction on the studio full steam ahead, and Sidney working long hours, her creativity had come to a screeching halt, and it concerned her.

Lying there in the sun with the waves lapping against the pier she began to talk to God. *Father, You are the keeper of my soul, You know my heart, I've so much to be thankful for, my family, my home, my talent and yet lately I feel anxious like I'm not doing what You want me to do. I want to be your servant God, am I missing something? I know I've been upset about Sidney working so much, am I just being selfish? And now here we are the three of us together, and I still feel uneasy. Give me peace Lord, take away my fears. Show me the way. I love you God, thank you for the blessings and thank you for loving me. In Jesus' Name. Amen*

"Hey, are you asleep over there, look at what your son has built. He says it looks like the playhouse we are building in the back," Sidney said smiling at the thought that Ryan was going to use the studio as a playhouse.

"That's a good job, Ryan," she said leaning on one elbow to see the sand building. "Are you two getting hungry, I have some sandwiches and juice in the cooler."

"Look, mom, I can make a slide from my bedroom window down to the playhouse. That will be fun?" Ryan said scooping up more sand to make a slide.

"I don't know about that Ryan. It looks pretty dangerous to me. Can you see the studio from your window?" Leslie said concerned.

"Yes. I watch those men working from my window," he said continuing to build a slide out of the wet sand.

"How about we eat, I'm really getting hungry over here all by myself on the blanket," Leslie said pulling the cooler next to her.

Leslie's cell phone began to ring and looking at the screen she said to Sidney, "its Jeffrey."

"Hello Jeffrey. How are you on this beautiful day?"

"I'm doing well, and you?"

"Well, right now the three Rye's are on the beach up the coast for an outing. What can I do for you," Leslie said wondering why Jeffrey was calling her.

He explained his concerns about Nick, the GC his sister had hired. "Annabelle suggested you could do some research and, if you have time, to see what you could find out about him, I would appreciate it. Also, I was wondering if you and Sidney would be available to help me, Annabelle, and Katrina Louise clear out the folk's house so she could get started on the repairs and upgrades," Jeffrey said.

Leslie told him she would be glad to do the research and asked him to email her any info he may have on Nick. Then turning to Sidney, the phone muted, she asked him if he would have time to help.

"I don't know Les, we are really snowed under, it was hard enough to have time to spend with you and Ryan," Sidney told her as she unmuted the phone.

"Jeffrey, Sidney is pretty busy right now, but I'll be glad to help any way I can," she said with a little sadness that Sidney couldn't help too.

After lunch, they packed everything up, and with one last look at the ocean, they loaded the car and headed back home. Leslie watched as the shoreline disappeared. *What a lovely time spent with family,* she thought. Perhaps this outing would get her back on track writing her latest book.

Chapter **3**

"We'll just give the kitchen utensils to the thrift store. Leslie, if you see anything you think I might want to keep, please put it aside. I've gone through most of it, but I may have missed something, you know like anything with a wooden handle or wrought iron, that sort of thing," Katrina Louise explained.

"I'll do my best. But you are basically saying anything that is really old?" Leslie said not wanting the responsibility of identifying any heirlooms.

Nodding her head, Katrina Louise went upstairs to sort through the linens.

Everything was cleared out of the parlor, so Nick was taking down the light fixtures from the area around the mantel and the chandelier on the ceiling to be cleaned.

With Nick out of earshot, Leslie asked Jeffrey to come closer. "I've looked into Nick's past, but there seems to be some missing parts, dates, timelines that sort of thing,"

"Is that unusual?" Jeffrey asked as Leslie handed him a handful of cooking utensils that he put in a box.

"Could be. But, don't worry I've just started. There could be more. I'll let you know."

"Thank you, Leslie, for doing this for me," he said lending a hand to help her get on the step stool to reach dishes in the upper cabinet.

"Your welcome, I'll hand these to you while you wrap that paper over there around them and put them in another box."

Just then from the other room, Nick called to Jeffrey. "I could use some help with this monster of a chandelier. It's really awkward and heavy. I sure don't want to drop it."

With a nod from Leslie letting him know it was alright, Jeffrey headed to the parlor where he found Nick on a very high ladder. "If you'll hold the ladder steady, I'll wrestle this monster collection of crystals," Nick called down to him.

Jeffrey grabbed the sides of the ladder and, balancing his body, steadied the very tall structure as he watched Nick slowly descend toward the floor. The crystals banged against each other making a ringing noise that brought Katrina Louise downstairs to investigate. Watching from the doorway, she held her breath until Nick was near the last rung of the ladder. Then she rushed to help protect the crystals as slowly they were laid on the floor.

"Nick, that could have been a disaster. You should not have done this alone. What were you thinking? This thing probably weighs close to 500 pounds not to mention the fact that it is a selling point in this house. You really need to build some scaffolding for these twenty-foot ceilings. Now that it is down here what do you suggest we do with it?" Katrina Louise scolded.

"That's your problem, lady. You are the one who wanted it cleaned," he said coming off the ladder.

"If you had the scaffolding up, it could be hung from it while we take the crystals off, but now it is laying on the floor, and hopefully not one of these very expensive crystals are broken. Nothing else can be done in here until the scaffolding is installed. Understood?"

"Yes, Ma'am, my wish is your command," he said tipping his hat at her as she left the room.

"Do you really want this job?" Jeffrey asked fed up with Nick's attitude.

"I'm not sure," Nick answered trying to hide his embarrassment.

"If you do, I would change that tone. I warned you about that before. Katrina Louise won't put up with it nor should she. So, get a grip and do what she asked." Jeffrey said frustrated with Nick's inability to take orders from a woman. If a man had told him the same thing, it would be a different story. He truly hoped this relationship between Nick and Katrina Louise would somehow work out.

Leslie waited in the kitchen and listened to Jeffrey talk to Nick. Impressed with what he said on the one hand but concerned on the other hand because of Nick's apparent lack of character. She had misgivings about him from the first introduction when Nick deliberately gave her the once over making her feel extremely uncomfortable. No wonder Jeffrey asked her to check his background. It appeared Jeffrey had reservations too. She wondered if Katrina Louise felt the same way or did she think she could handle the situation? Whichever the case, Leslie intended to find out more about this unsavory character and soon.

Chapter **4**

"How was your day at the French Market? Any more progress on the jewelry ring?" Leslie asked Sidney while they prepared dinner.

"No," Sidney said taking a bite of carrots as Leslie cut them in strips. "Things have come to a standstill. I put Charles on another case that came in yesterday. I can handle this one for the time being until something breaks in the investigation."

"Well, I had an interesting day."

"Do tell me more," Sidney said giving her a side hug.

"I went to the Bordeaux House to help Katrina Louise. Jeffrey was there, and he introduced me to this Nick character. I don't like him at all, he has an ego as big as all outdoors and thinks he is God's gift to women. You know the kind of man I'm talking about Sidney. The kind of man you wouldn't want your sister around."

"Or my wife."

"Anyway, I'm not sure Katrina Louise should keep this guy working for her, and I would for sure be sad if anything happened to her. I told Jeffrey I couldn't find much information on Nick but would certainly dig deeper if necessary."

"Is he doing good work?" Sidney asked.

"Not really, Katrina Louise got on him for not putting up scaffolding before he took a very expensive chandelier down in the parlor. It was heavy. He yelled for Jeffrey to help him. Then Katrina Louise came to save the crystals as they dropped to the floor. She told him not to do any more work in the parlor until the scaffolding was installed."

"Sounds like she knows what she is doing. The question is, does Nick. I don't want you over there without Jeffrey or me. I just don't like the sound of it," Sidney said handing down the plates from the upper cabinets.

"That's okay by me. I don't want to be there by myself, and we should tell Jeffrey so he can tell Katrina Louise."

"Let's wait until you have had more time to run a more thorough background check on Nick."

*****

Katrina Louise walked around the house checking on the work Nick was doing. She was becoming increasingly skeptical concerning his skills. She was desperate to get this project done, however, if she kept Nick on as GC it may end up costing more than she intended to invest. *Decisions, decisions, well that is the name of the game Katrine Louise so quit your grumbling.* She thought.

Suddenly she heard a creak like someone walking on a loose floorboard. Taking a deep breath, she turned around. Standing in front of her, clean shaven, clean clothes was Nick, the object of her decision.

"Are you in the habit of sneaking up on people?" she said aware of his new persona.

"I saw your car out front, and since it is Sunday, I wondered why you were here, is all," Nick said keeping his distance.

"May I ask what your new look is all about. Did you attend church?" she said then continued. "Perhaps a new girl?"

"Can't a man cleanup once in a while?"

Katrina Louise found herself attracted to this new Nick and it unnerved her. *What is his game?* She wondered. "You haven't answered my question."

"Tell me, is that part of the job description, Ms. Bordeaux, or are you just being noisy?" he said with a familiar smirk on his face.

For the first time in an extremely long time, she asked God to protect her. She could feel her heart pounding in fear dispelling any attraction she felt earlier. She swallowed then told him. "I'm meeting my brother here to go over some decisions I've made, he should be here soon," she said hoping he didn't sense her fear.

"Well then, I better be on my way. I'll be here in the morning, bright and early," he said leaving the room and walking out the front door.

She took deep breaths trying to regain her composure, then went to the front window making sure he left. Just then he turned and waved to her standing in the window. *What am I going to do now? Will he retaliate if I let him go? Oh, I know he is busy, but I wish Jean-Paul could take this on.* She told herself as she felt her body begin to shake. In all her years selling real estate, this was the first time she felt threatened.

Chapter **5**

Jeffrey and Annabelle walked to the square from Sully's drugstore after their prayer meeting. The French Quarter had an air of celebration as the atmosphere surrounded them. They decided to have breakfast at Café Du Monde. The waiter seated them close to the outside of the area under the canopy. They ordered coffee with chicory and began to read the menu. Across the street, Annabelle spotted Leslie and Sidney walking with their little boy.

"Look, Jeffrey, it's the Rye family," she said waving.

Sidney led his family across the street and up to their table. "Hey, you two, enjoying this beautiful weather?"

"Come join us," Jeffrey said. "We can get a bigger table."

"Glad too, but we are headed for a paddle boat ride on the river," Sidney said. "We thought Ryan would enjoy it."

"What a wonderful idea," Annabelle said. Then to Ryan, she asked. "Are you going to ride on a boat?"

He wiggled, then said, "A paddle boat."

Just then Jeffrey's cell went off.

"Hello."

"Wait a minute, slow down Sis. I can't understand you."

Annabelle looked at Jeffrey concerned, and Ryan pulled at Sidney trying to make him keep walking. Leslie's radar went up as she came closer to the table.

"What is it?" Leslie questioned.

"That was Katrina Louise. She just had an encounter with Nick that unnerved her. She wanted to tell me about it. It seems he cleaned himself up and came to the folk's place unexpectedly while she was there looking over his work. She sounded frightened," Jeffrey told them.

"Is she alright?" Annabelle asked.

"I think so. She said she would call me later."

"This doesn't make sense. What did she mean by 'he cleaned himself up'?" Leslie said.

"Just that he had cleaned up his beard and pulled his hair back in a ponytail, and he was wearing a sports jacket and slacks."

"Maybe he had a date," Annabelle said.

"I don't know, maybe. She was just surprised when he came in. But, she is generally in control of the situation. It sounded as if she was not in control this time. I'll talk with her later and see what's going on," he said.

"Well, let us know, we better get this boy on the boat before it takes off down the river. So we'll see you later. Call if we can help in any way," Sidney said letting Ryan pull him away.

The sun was minutes away from creating a beautiful sunset as they walked back toward the square from the boat dock. Ryan was fast asleep on Sidney's shoulder. "I don't like what happened with Jeffrey's sister today. She doesn't appear to be an alarmist. A very controlled person, it surprises me that she would be frightened by Nick unless he gave her reason. I just have a gut feeling about all of this," Leslie said as they got in the taxi headed for home.

"If you feel uneasy then maybe you ought to make some excuse not to be over there. In any case, you shouldn't be there by yourself," Sidney said keeping his voice down so as not to wake Ryan.

Later that night after a long day in the French Quarter and on the paddle boat with Ryan, she was finally able to check her laptop for information about Nick. Still not finding much to go on. She tried to find him under different names. *Nothing. I'm just too tired. I'll do it tomorrow.* Then bowing in prayer: *Father, thank you for a beautiful day with my family. Lord thank you for our little guy, Ryan. And, dear Lord, keep Katrina Louise safe and help me find out more about Nick. In Jesus' Name. Amen*

*****

Monday morning found Sidney back at his observation in the French Market. He walked around first as a customer and later as a vendor all the time keeping his eye out for unusual activity. Over the course of several weeks, he had observed the coming and going of the same two or three men. Sometimes in pairs and sometimes alone. However, today there was a new face on the block that seemed to be in charge. He watched while the men appeared in deep conversation leaning in to listen to what the new man was saying and making sure no one else could hear them. It was times like this Sidney wished he could read lips.

Not wanting to draw attention, he casually positioned himself closer, all the time adjusting the merchandise in front of him, to appear like the vendor for that area. Suddenly the men turned and left, walking toward the area where the jewelry was sold. Before Sidney could make the transition, they were gone. He looked out over the parking area, but he had no luck spotting them. He had a good look at the new man and was sure he would see him at the market again. Meanwhile, he would keep up his surveillance.

His client, a well-known insurance agent in the French Quarter, hired Sidney when some of his clients reported their jewelry missing. They reported it to the police but there was nothing to go on, and there was some suspicious activity at the French Market to warrant an investigation.

Sidney's thought, *How and why did they pick the French Market to fence their goods*. So far, nothing stood out except for these men who frequented the market without a distinct purpose. He was convinced that time would expose their activity. He just needed to be patient.

"Hi, Les, do you think you can break away long enough to meet me for lunch at the po'boy's place close to the market?"

"Sure, I'm on my way," Leslie said closing her laptop, checking with the nanny, Daisy, then calling a taxi.

Arriving in the French Quarter, she walked to the market hoping Sidney was still there. Not finding him she went on to the local hangout. Leslie was hungry for a Shrimp po'boy. Seeing two sandwiches on the counter where Sidney sat, she realized he had read her mind and order the same thing for both of them.

"Oh, Sid, you know me so well," she said leaning over for a kiss.

"How are things on the home front? Are you getting anything accomplished?"

"Well, sort of, I've been searching for Jeffrey's subject with no luck. It's like the guy dropped into the French Quarter from the sky."

"Have you talked to Jeffrey about Katrina Louise's encounter yesterday?"

"Actually, I talked to Katrina Louise. I was concerned about her and wanted to make sure her reaction was real, you know, not out of surprise. She assured me it was real. She confessed to being attracted to him at first when she saw what he looked like cleaned up. However, that attraction turned quickly to uneasiness when he seemed to be coming on to her. The clincher was when she went to the front window to make sure he was leaving, and he turned and waved to her like he expected her to be there. That really scared her." Leslie said stopping long enough to take a bite of the po'boy.

"So, your intuitions were right. Do you think she will allow him to stay on as the GC?"

"She said she was afraid of what he may do if she fired him. So, she and Jeffrey talked about it, and she doesn't plan to go over to the house unless someone is with her," Leslie said patting her mouth with a napkin.

"What about the references that Katrina Louise checked? I thought she said they were okay," Sidney said.

"I asked her about that, and she said all his references were recent, none were any older than two years ago," Leslie told Sidney.

"But, they were good references, or she wouldn't have hired him, right?"

"That was my thought too."

They finished their meal, then Sidney walked her back to the French Market where she called a taxi. On the way back to the Garden District, her mind churned ideas as she tried to come up with answers to the many questions about Nick.

The Following day, Jeffrey called and asked Leslie if she was available to help him at his folk's house. He told Katrina Louise that he would finish unloading the kitchen and would like it if Leslie could help him. Arrangements made with the nanny, Leslie waited for Jeffrey to give her a ride to the house. While alone in the car, they discussed the reality of Nick's missing past.

"I'm still trying to find information under another name. I wish I knew where he was before he came here. That would help a lot. Next time you have a chance to have a conversation with him, perhaps you can get him to talk about it," Leslie suggested.

"I'll give it a try, but he's now aware of my issues with him, and he may not open up, but no harm in trying," Jeffrey told her.

While Leslie and Jeffrey worked in the kitchen, Nick put up the scaffolding in the dining room so he could take down another chandelier. Surprised when the back door leading to the kitchen opened, they both turned around and said hello to Katrina Louise.

"I thought I would come by and see how you two are doing. How are things going? It looks like you have gotten a lot done. I do appreciate your help with this. I had no idea what an undertaking it would become," Katrina Louise said looking around the kitchen at the empty cabinets and pantry. "I guess the butler's pantry is next. Then, I can pick out the paint colors. I want it to look fresh but stay in the flavor of the original."

"I remember how much fun we had when it came to picking paint colors, but keeping the colors authentic was a real challenge," Leslie said handing a platter to Jeffrey.

"That's right, you and your husband renovated your Garden District home. Was it also designed by Gallier?" Katrina Louise said wondering if they kept the Greek revival style.

"Yes. We wanted to keep the same style which meant a lot of trips to the library to check out books on that era, and also we found several books on Gallier, which were interesting."

"Gallier Hall, over on Royal was one of his designs wasn't it?" Jeffrey said.

"Why, brother, you surprise me. I didn't know you were into history."

"There are probably a lot of things about me you don't know," he said giving her a big grin.

"Well, as long as we're discussing history, here are some facts we discovered. Gallier Hall originally was his and his second wife, Catherine's, home. It later became City Hall. Then it was named Gallier Hall after James Gallier Sr. You've heard of the tragedy when the Steamboat, *Evening Star,* was lost during a hurricane off the coast of South Carolina on its way to New York. Well, the Galliers were onboard when the luxury steamer went down. Gallier and his wife, Catherine, both perished," Leslie told her captive audience.

"Thank you, Leslie, for the history lesson. Stories like that help sell these old houses. My clients eat it up," Katrina Louise said helping Leslie step down from the stool.

"Even though that happened a long time ago, back in the 1800s, Gallier Hall is still a major tourist attraction because of the architecture," Leslie continued. "So, James Gallier Sr. has a legacy that carries on right here in New Orleans."

"I just had an idea. I can have a plaque made with all his information on it, and hang it by the front door," Katrina Louise said excitedly.

All the talk about Gallier had kept the three others occupied, and Nick took this opportunity to do some snooping. He went upstairs to the bedrooms and searched through drawers and closets looking for anything of value. It seemed to have already been picked clean, but he kept searching. Entering the largest bedroom, he pulled drawers from the marble-topped nightstands next to the large bed in the middle of the room. *People actually lived here.* He said to himself. Then hearing footsteps on the stairs, he turned and looked up at the ceiling.

"What are you doing in here?" Jeffrey asked after coming to look for Nick when Katrina Louise couldn't find him downstairs.

"Just checking to see if I need any more scaffolding," Nick said not missing a beat.

"Well, Katrina Louise wants to talk to you downstairs," Jeffrey said leading the way down the back stairs leading to the kitchen.

"I hear you want to talk to me," Nick said stepping into the kitchen.

"I was getting ready to leave and wanted to go over the schedule for tomorrow. I see the scaffolding is up in the dining room, so you can start there. Will you need any help with the chandelier?"

"I think I can manage. If I need any help I have a friend who can come," Nick said waiting for her reaction.

"Actually, I have a plumber coming tomorrow, first thing, so he will be able to help you if need be. His name is Benny. He takes care of all my plumbing needs. I'll let him know. He will probably be here most of the day working in the bathrooms and kitchen putting in new fixtures," she said as a matter of fact.

"New fixtures? Won't that take away from the style of the house?"

"These fixtures are salvaged from other houses this style."

Nick nodded in agreement and went back to the dining room to collect his tools before leaving for the day.

"I'll lock up after everyone is out," Jeffrey said giving Katrina Louise a hug and walking her to the back door.

"Thank you, Jeffrey. And thank you too, Leslie. Can I give you a ride back to your place?"

"Oh yes. Thank you. I really need to get home, so the nanny can leave," Leslie said telling Jeffrey goodbye.

Jeffrey hung around waiting on Nick. He was looking in the Butler's Pantry when Nick came up and stood in the doorway. "Well, shall we call it a day Mr. Bordeaux?"

"I'm ready if you are," Jeffrey said following Nick to the back door. After locking the door behind them, the two men walked down the driveway neither saying a word. When they reached their cars, Nick called to Jeffrey.

"See you tomorrow."

Jeffrey waved and got into his car. He sat a while and waited for Nick to leave. Then called Annabelle at her office.

"Hi, I'm going to run by my office for a while, can we make a date for dinner later at our favorite place?"

"Sounds good. I have a lot of work so later would be great. Do you want to meet there say around eight or do you want to pick me up since you have your car?"

"I'll pick you up. How does a quarter til sound?"

"That'll work for me. I love you. See you then," Annabelle said.

"I love you too," Jeffrey said then pulled out of the driveway onto St. Charles Ave. Out of habit he checked his rearview mirror and was surprised to see Nick's pickup following a couple of car links behind him. *I thought he left ahead of me. You're just being paranoid.* He told himself all the time watching his mirror to see if the truck would turn off onto another street. Soon Jeffrey made the green light just as it turned yellow and the pickup stopped. Relieved that Nick was not following him, Jeffrey headed for his office.

"Are you sure it wasn't another pickup that looked like his?" Annabelle asked across the table.

"I'm probably just paranoid. All this worry about Sis and Nick has me a little unnerved. She was looking for him today and couldn't find him. I found him upstairs in the folk's master bedroom. Said he was seeing if the room needs scaffolding. I didn't believe him for a minute. He had no business being upstairs." Jeffrey said frustrated.

"This is really bothering you, Jeffrey. Has Leslie found out anything about Nick yet?"

"She said she can't find anything about him before he came to the French Quarter. She wanted me to see if I could find out where he was before coming here. But, I didn't have a chance to talk to him alone, or maybe I'm afraid to ask him for fear he will get suspicious. I didn't care for the guy from the start, and now I wish I had talked Katrina Louise out of hiring him."

"Well, not to change the subject, but I have some news that might cheer you up," Annabelle said reaching across the table for his hand. "I called to see about our wedding reception at Gallier Hall in the pink room. It will hold up to one hundred people and…" Annabelle stopped noting Jeffrey's expression. "You don't like the idea?"

"It's not that. It's just a coincidence. Leslie gave us a history lesson on Gallier Hall today. Did you know that Gallier Sr. and his wife perished on the Steamboat, *Evening Star,* during a hurricane on their way to New York?"

Annabelle lowered her head and looking at Jeffrey quizzingly removed her hand from his. "And this is why you are looking at me like this isn't a good idea? Have you ever seen the pink room at Gallier Hall? It has beautiful chandeliers… three I think. I just thought it would be a fun, beautiful place to celebrate our wedding with a reception for our family and friends."

"You're right, forgive me. How soon do we need to let them know?"

"They are booked through June with graduations, weddings and such."

"So, we wouldn't get married until July?" Jeffrey said confused.

"That would give us plenty of time to plan the wedding and the reception."

"I thought we were just going to have a quiet ceremony?

"We can but somewhere romantic, somewhere surrounded by greenery, lights and a fountain. I've been looking at venues for weddings in the French Quarter, and Jeffrey the places are breathtaking. Don't you want it to be special?"

Jeffrey found his head beginning to ache. Their meal came and bowing their heads they blessed the food. Jeffrey held on to Annabelle's hands after the prayer and looking her in the eye, he told her. "This is our day, and yes, I want it to be special. I want us to plan it together but most of all I want you to be happy." Annabelle didn't tell Jeffrey she put her name on the waiting list hoping for an earlier date. *Best leave things alone for now.* She thought.

This was a side of Annabelle he had not seen before, almost like a little girl waiting for Christmas morning. Her excitement was almost overwhelming. As they ate in silence, he began to pray for guidance. *Father, the keeper of my heart, help me understand this woman I love so dearly. Please give me the words to say and take away any anxiety I may have about the plans for our wedding. And Lord almighty, help me with Nick. I seem to be lost in my feelings there Lord, help me do and say the right things and be there for Annabelle and my sister. In His precious name. Amen.*

"Are you alright?"

"Yes, I'm getting a bit of a headache, perhaps if I eat I'll feel better," Jeffrey said quite honestly but not revealing his misgivings, not only about the wedding plans but about his sister's involvement with his family's home. It dawned on him that she had not told the other siblings that she bought their parent's house and was renovating it to sell. His connection in the whole process made him feel uneasy. How could he explain his involvement with Katrina Louise and the house? Just the thought of bringing more grief to his family upset him. When he thought back about the months of uncertainty around his brother Jonathon and the hurt it brought to all the siblings, he was sure this thing with his sister was about to get really complicated.

Chapter **6**

Ignoring the buzzing of the cell phone, Leslie continued typing, her ideas filling the screen. She was out of her slump and wanted to keep writing while it was flowing on the page. The buzzing started again, and without taking her fingers off the keyboard, she glanced at the cell phone to make sure it wasn't Sidney then she continued. She noted that she would call Annabelle back when she was at a stopping point. Thirty minutes passed, and the buzzing began again.

"Hello," Leslie said setting the cell phone beside her laptop.

"Leslie, I'm so scared," Annabelle said, holding back tears.

"Want's wrong?" Leslie said picking the cell phone up from the desk.

"It's Jeffrey. I think he has changed his mind about the wedding."

"Why would you think that? Has something happened?" Leslie questioned.

Annabelle began to tell her friend about Gallier Hall and waiting until July to get married and Jeffrey's reaction.

"He said he had a headache, but Leslie I think he was…well, surprised or uneasy. I don't know he was just different and it changed the atmosphere of the rest of the evening. When he took me home, he said he didn't want to come up to my place because he had a busy day ahead," Annabelle said between sobs.

"Annabelle, he said he had a headache, and maybe he was just tired. He has been spending a lot of time helping Katrina Louise. That has probably put him behind in his own work. I know I'm a little behind and I haven't spent half as much time as he has, helping her. Besides that, he is worried about the situation. I'm sure he just wasn't ready to talk about all the wedding plans right at that moment."

"Oh, Leslie, do you really think that is what happened?" Annabelle said stroking Phoebe's head while she sat on her lap.

"Well, you know how you get excited about things. Perhaps Jeffrey couldn't get as excited, because you did it without him. Sometimes our men like to be included. If it were me, I would apologize for not talking to him first before calling Gallier Hall. Maybe that's what upset him," Leslie told her.

"He did say he wanted us to make plans together. Your right, Leslie. He probably just wants to be included, and I made him feel left out. Thank you, you always make me feel better. I guess that's because you know me so well," Annabelle said then they said their goodbyes.

She put Phoebe down and the second she was on the floor Annabelle went to the kitchen and poured her a bowl of dog food.

Losing the original Phoebe had been very hard. But when Sidney found another dog that looked just like her beloved poodle, she jumped at the chance to have her and named her Phoebe, also.

*****

Before she could return to her work, Leslie thought about Annabelle. She had noticed lately that her friend wasn't her usual self. She chalked it up to Annabelle being overwhelmed about getting married again, but her intuition was telling her something else was wrong. She determined to spend more one-on-one time with Annabelle, and maybe that would shed some light on the underlying cause of the change she had observed.

Annabelle sat at her desk staring at nothing in particular as she thought about what Leslie said. She wondered why she felt the need to push her thoughts about the wedding on Jeffrey. He gave her no reason to feel as if she couldn't share with him. Did it have something to do with her letting go of her deceased husband Dean? She was sure she had left that behind, however, she didn't understand her rush to make these decisions about their wedding on her own. Maybe it was the attorney in her, or maybe it was just her personality bringing out her independent side. She wanted a life with Jeffrey, she wanted to share her life with him, but was her autonomous nature going to ruin it for them? These thoughts filled her head as she tried to figure out what had happened between them. She had never felt estranged from him before, and it still worried her. She bowed her head in prayer. *Heavenly Father, I trust you with my thoughts and actions. Thank you for the peace you give me when I trust you to provide answers and guidance. I recognize the fact that when I don't keep you at the center of my life, things begin to fall apart. Forgive me, Lord, Your love is sufficient to take away my anxiety. I love you Lord, and I'm grateful for your love. In His precious name. Amen.*

She picked up the phone and dialed Jeffrey's number. Waiting for him to answer, she asked God to help her say the right thing.

"Hi Annabelle, I was just getting ready to call you. Great minds work together, so they say," Jeffrey said.

"Are you busy right now?"

"No. I was at a stopping point, that's why I wanted to talk to you. I didn't realize how behind I was getting, after spending so much time helping Katrina Louise."

"I'm so sorry Jeffrey that I didn't realize how hard it had been for you to help your sister on top of your concern about the man she hired. I didn't mean to burden you with a wedding decision. And Jeffrey, you're right. It is our wedding, and I do want to plan it together. Do you forgive me?"

"Sweetheart, don't give it another thought. I'm sorry I didn't see how excited you have been about the wedding. I've been so wrapped up in the folk's house and decisions my sister is making, not to mention being concerned about what the family will say when they find out what she has done and that I'm involved," Jeffrey said.

"Oh Jeffrey, I wasn't aware she hasn't told your family she bought the house. I'm sorry I haven't been there for you. But I am now, and I want you to know you can count on me. Is there anything I can do to make things easier for you?" Annabelle said with tears coming to the surface. "Both of us need to remember who is really in charge."

"How right you are. Let's put it in God's hands. Prayer certainly helps, doesn't it?" Jeffrey said remembering that Annabelle brought him, through prayer groups, into a closer relationship with God.

"Yes. We are human and forget to keep Him at the center of everything we do but going forward we will remember. Our marriage will be built on a firm footing with God in control. I love you, and I want the best for us, and with God's help it will happen," Annabelle said with conviction.

They both were in a better place when the conversation ended. Jeffrey told Annabelle he would insist that Katrina Louise tell the family what she had done, and he would take responsibility for his part. This would take some of the pressure from him, so he could spend more time with her making wedding plans. They agreed their conversation had helped both of them and they would keep open communication going forward.

Chapter 7

Her plan was to invite everyone to have lunch at Galatoir's on Bourbon Street. She knew the ladies would be excited and the gentlemen would go along out of courtesy. It would cost her plenty but would also give the family a chance to be together again on a social base rather than sitting in Annabelle's office listening to all the bad news around the loss of the Bordeaux's Trust Fund. After all, the Bordeaux family was one of the most well-known aristocratic families of the day. The Bordeaux legacy went back several generations, and even though their brother Jonathon came close to destroying their family reputation, it was time to move on.

"So, what do you think?" Katrina Louise waited for her brother's reaction.

"I think it sounds very extravagant. Why would you want to spend that kind of money just to tell the family about you buying the folk's house? Do you plan to share the profit with them or are you going to pocket the money yourself? And, how do you think they will feel about you not including them in the process? Sis, you are treading on a slippery slope. You realize that one of the stipulations of Jonathon's release from charges was to pay back the money taken from the Trust. How is he going to feel when you tell him about your plan to flip the house for a profit? Don't you think he would have wanted to at least be given the opportunity to help so he could recoup some of the money?" Jeffrey said in desperation.

"Wait just a minute, big brother. I put my hard-earned money in the purchase of this house, and my money will pay any of the expenses going forward. Why should I split the profit with anyone?" she said on the defense.

"All I'm saying is maybe there is another way. And you have been worried all along about how the siblings would take the fact you bought their family home without one thought about them individually or collectively. The way I see it, you need to make a decision. Are they in? Or are you cutting them out?"

"I can't see a way that is fair for everyone," she said feeling ashamed.

"How's this? You tell them you took the opportunity to purchase the house knowing, with some elbow grease, it could potentially turn a nice profit. But, if all the work has to be hired out to someone else, then that would dig into the profit. However, if everyone pitched in and helped with the work that needs to be done, then they could share in the larger profit margin thus making each share larger. That would certainly get their attention, and I dare say they would be more than willing to help if they are working for a return from their efforts. All of this would need to be in writing, and I'm sure we could count on Annabelle to draw up the papers. Besides, that may be a way to let Nick go."

"You're right, Jeffrey. Your plan just may work. Do you think we could have the meeting in Annabelle's office? With her there it would keep things from getting out of hand and she might make some suggestions on the legal side of everything," Katrina Louise said once she realized how selfish she was being. "And getting rid of Nick would undoubtedly be an added bonus.

"I'll discuss it with her tonight. She may shed some light of her own on this plan. As an attorney, she can make it fair for everyone and make sure Jonathon's share goes toward his obligation with the courts."

Satisfied with the plan they ended their conversation and agreed to talk later. Jeffrey had a sigh of relief, and he recognized God had given him a way to help everyone. *Thank you, Lord. My faith is in you, and I accept your promise to always be there. My words to Katrina Louise came from you, Lord. I'm so grateful for your help. I pray for my family going forward for their understanding and acceptance. In Jesus' Name. Amen.*

Chapter **8**

Sidney's presence in the French Market was becoming too obvious, so he arranged with the organizers of the market to become a vendor. After Leslie did some research on a product he could sell, he rented space and set up shop not far from one of the booths selling jewelry. This particular space had seemed most likely to be selling stolen goods. It was close to an exit providing a quick get-a-way. Even though other vendors were buying and selling jewelry he had his eye on this one all along.

It had been a while since he saw the strange individual come into the market but the others that were with the stranger that day were still involved in the operation. He was sure they were bringing in stolen goods. He planned to strike up a conversation with his new neighbors hoping one of them may slip or even suggest he get in on the action.

While setting up his space, he watched the two men go in and out never looking his way. After a couple of days, Sidney finished making the area presentable and said hello to the man left behind to run the booth. The only response was a slight nod of the head as the short older bald-headed man turned away pretending to arrange the jewelry on the display. Sidney began to fold the scarfs on his table all the time watching. When the man turned back around Sidney was to close to be ignored, and the man commented on Sidney's display.

"It's looking nice. You may even get some customers," he said.

"I certainly hope so. My old lady will not be happy if I don't make some money after investing in these confined scarves and the rent on this space. Can you believe how much they get for this space? Maybe we're in the wrong business. We could make a lot more money collecting rent," Sidney quipped trying to get some input and a little sympathy hoping to get on his good side.

The little man didn't take the bait and turned back around when a customer came up. Sidney overheard him doing a real sales job on the unsuspecting girl.

*****

Annabelle felt a sense of dread come over her thinking about her conversation with Katrina Louise. Like Jeffrey, she desperately wanted to move on from the hurt, confusion, brokenness that surrounded the Bordeaux family for so long. She knew how this adventure of Jeffrey's sister was monopolizing his time and energy. Perhaps this idea of his would serve to appease some if not all of his siblings.

Reluctantly, she agreed to have the family meet at her office so Katrina Louise could explain the plan she and Jeffrey had come up with. That night while she and Jeffrey talked about their wedding plans he asked her about the upcoming meeting.

"Are you alright with this?"

"Yes, I was a little apprehensive at first, but I thought about Jonathon and how it would help him. I spent a lot of time with him while he was in jail and on trial and I grew to like him and understand why he did what he did. A very cunning woman duped him at a very vulnerable stage in his life. I believe he deserves better than that and I pray your sisters can put their feelings aside and give him a chance to redeem himself," Annabelle said quite seriously.

"You sound like his lawyer pleading his case," Jeffrey said smiling at her.

"In a way I guess I'll always plead his case especially with A.J. Your youngest sister is not ready for any kind of forgiveness towards him. Rose Marie, on the other hand, never gave up hope. She stayed on his side from the beginning, never wavering even when it looked like the deck was stacked against him. Most likely, it was the light your oldest sister shed on the whole situation that saved him in the end."

"Yes, and I wonder how A.J. will handle this. She doesn't do well when it comes to thinking about anyone other than herself. Maybe when she accepts the fact that she may actually get some money, after all, she may be willing to work for it."

"Are you serious? I can't imagine A.J. working for anything. This will be a real shock to her system. But maybe you are right. She might be able to see the light at the end of her tunnel if she goes along with this. We'll see," Annabelle said shaking her head in disbelief.

When the day arrived for the meeting at Annabell's office, she asked God to help the family to be receptive to Katrina Louise's plan for their future. As one by one they began to arrive, Annabelle, standing in front of her desk greeted each one and smiled, showing them they had nothing to worry about. When Jonathon arrived, she gave him her own personal assurance that everything was okay.

She had arranged the seating in a circle, and she sat down in one of the seats next to Jeffrey. Then with a smile, she turned the meeting over to their sister Katrina Louise who stayed seated.

"I'm so glad everyone could make it today because I have some exciting news to tell you. This could change our future and hopefully bring us all closer together," she said in spite of the nervousness apparent in her voice. Looking at Jeffrey, she continued. "Please hold your reactions to what I'm going to say until I finish. Our childhood home went on the market recently as a quick sale by the bank that held the mortgage and … well, I purchased it," in spite of the sudden reactions from those in the room, she continued. "As you might imagine if you haven't seen the house lately it's in dire need of repair and clean up inside and out. That's where each of you come in. I propose that we, together, renovate the place to resell for a profit. It would mean each of us would have to put in hard labor and long hours, but we could get a rather nice profit to divide among us," she said, then looking at Jonathon. "This would help you with the court, and we all could see a return on the investment."

A.J. raised her hand like a school girl. When Katrina Louise recognized her hand in the air, A.J. asked. "So are you saying we would have to work for the money we were going to get from our inheritance?"

"I'm saying this is an opportunity for us to recoup some of the money lost. We're talking about a healthy sum of money if we work hard at getting the place in good condition, even getting it back on the historical society register. A.J. you could come away with a share of the profit," Katrin Louise said.

"But, what could I do," she questioned.

"The grounds are in terrible shape. The fence needs repair and paint. The garden needs weeding and replanting. The galley needs repair and paint. There are a lot of things you can do. But in order to receive any money from the profit of selling the house, you will have to help. Do you understand that?"

"I guess so," A.J. said trying to figure out how hard this would be. After all, she was not use to doing any kind of labor, not even in her own home, let alone that big house, and she wasn't sure she would be able to work outside in the heat pulling weeds. She had lived a very privileged lifestyle on the money received for child support from two previous husbands. As the baby in the family, her folks had spoiled her with anything she wanted. She had never worked for money, and she had never done manual labor. She wanted the money but how was she going to get her share if she couldn't do the work?

Annabelle stifled her need to laugh as she watched A.J. trying to figure everything out. Jeffrey took her hand acknowledging the 'I told you so' look she gave him.

Chapter **9**

Not used to having trouble digging out information, Leslie went over again what she knew about Nick Nixon. Convinced that was not his real name she began to analyze the few things she could identify about him. Katrina Louise wanted Jean-Paul to help with her latest project. However, he was busy and couldn't get to it for a couple of months which would delay the sale of the house. So Jean-Paul gave her Nick's name. *That's it.* Leslie thought. *How did Jean-Paul know Nick?*

She would have to tread lightly as not to raise suspicion. Jean-Paul had also done work for her and Sidney on occasion. She decided to make up a story about thinking she may know Nick from somewhere and would he know where he worked before coming to New Orleans.

In order to have a reason, besides inquiries about Nick, she would ask him where to get the tile they used in their main house. She would tell him they wanted to use it in the studio and would he have time to lay the tile.

Her conversation was very productive. She got an address of sorts where Nick stayed over close to the river. Jean-Paul also gave her some names of his buddies that he hung around with. She began with tracking down his address. All she had was an area and maybe a place called The Bayou Manor where you could rent a room and get breakfast for less than half what you would pay for a hotel room. A call to The Bayou Manor confirmed that Nick Nixson lived there and, by all accounts, he was well liked by other people living there. In fact, the woman on the other end of the conversation told Leslie two or three of the men must work together because they left with Nick in his 'little red truck.' She shared with enthusiasm and never once asked why Leslie was asking all those questions. That thought did not satisfy Leslie as she recognized the busy-body would just as soon tell Nick about her conversation, especially if she was as attracted to him as Leslie suspected.

*****

With everyone on board Katrina Louise told Nick her family was going to be helping with things that she originally was going to have him do. She told him she would understand since his hours would be cut way back if he needed to find another project. Nick surprised her by saying he could stay around for a while as he looked for other work and he didn't mind his hours shortened. It just gave him more time to look.

Unknown to Katrina Louise, A.J. had stopped by earlier to see the place while Jeffrey was there. She was excited to meet the man her sister had hired to help with the work. Nick was certain he and A.J. were made from the same mold, and he intended to make her acquaintance. She let him know she was also interested, flirting the whole time she was there.

The interaction between them didn't go unnoticed by Jeffrey. He was glad Nick would be leaving. He knew his baby sister too well, and he didn't like the fact that she was giving Nick the come-on. Her sexy voice and the way she was dressed was a great embarrassment to him. It was obvious that Nick didn't care what Jeffrey saw or for that matter what he thought. Jeffrey just wished Leslie could come up with some information on this guy.

Chapter **10**

It had rained for days, and even with the humidity, it was nice to get out and walk around. They decided to stop at la Madeleine for a club sandwich since neither Annabelle nor Jeffrey was very hungry. Jeffrey held Phoebe's leash, and Annabelle had her arm wrapped tightly around Jeffrey's arm as they strolled the sidewalk and waved at the shopkeepers standing outside. A sense of belonging, of protection, of love, came over Annabelle as the sky began to put on a spectacular show of colors brought on by the end of the rain.

"I've heard it said, that after flooding the earth, God sent a rainbow and tonight he has sent us two. Is'nt that a special blessing?" Jeffrey said patting her hand on his arm.

"Yes. I love the moments when God sends us gifts…like little God moments to remind us of his vastness, his glory, and his power. Here we're walking on concrete surround by decadent buildings when all of a sudden he sends us rainbows. *Thank You, Father*," Annabelle said smiling as she and Jeffrey stopped to take it in. The rainbows arced behind the St. Louis Cathedral that was casting shadows on the square in front of it. Others stopped to look at the unusual sight. Even Phoebe sat quietly looking up at the sky. Usually noisy, the French Quarter became eerily quiet as though time stood still.

"I don't know about you, but I have goosebumps up and down my arms, and my legs are even tingling," Annabelle said almost in a whisper.

"Me too," he said giving her hand a squeeze.

The sun set behind the cathedral and the rainbows disappeared. The moment in time vanished as the many familiar sounds returned filling the air. A lone trumpet cried out the blues, horses hoofs pulling carriages around the square click-clacked on the brick roads, and tambourines kept rhythm for dancers in the streets. The street lights illuminated the area. People returned to their routines putting God's gift behind.

Jeffrey went through the line for both of them while Annabelle sat outside under the awning with Phoebe. Still basking in their earlier experience, they ate in silence with Phoebe lying under the table on top of Annabelle's feet.

"I think the market is still open. You want to go look around," Jeffrey asked.

"Yes," Annabelle replied a little suspicious.

They walked a few blocks and went inside. There were still several vendors open, so they began to look around. They came upon a jewelry booth and stopped to look.

"I haven't gotten you a ring yet. Do you see any you like?"

"That one with the sapphire. That's my birthstone."

The old man behind the counter pulled it out to show her. She put it on her finger, and it fit perfectly. She held her hand up to the light and then looked at Jeffrey.

"I really like this one."

Jeffrey gave him his credit card. As they left the market, Annabelle remarked that she knew a ring was why he wanted to go there all along.

"You want to know something else. I saw that same ring the other night when I was in here looking and I thought you would like it. By the way that was my mother's birthstone too," Jeffrey said holding her hand and moving the ring around on her finger.

"It's beautiful. I love it. Thank you, Jeffrey."

"So I guess this makes it official. We're engaged."

Chapter **11**

Ryan loved sitting across the table from Sidney, both working on their own project. He was concentrating on staying in the lines on his coloring book, while Sidney was deep in thought going over the papers in his briefcase.

"Did you draw that, Dad?" Ryan asked his father seeing the paper on the table.

"No, son. An artist drew it."

"Who is it?" Ryan asked looking at the man in the picture.

"Not sure."

"Why did the artist draw it?"

"It's someone I have been looking for?"

Ryan put his Crayola down and stared at his dad. His little mind tried to imagine the answer to his next question.

"Dad?"

"Yes, son," Sidney said without thinking knowing Ryan would ask more questions.

"If you are looking for this man in the picture, how do you know that is how he looks?"

"That's a good question, Ryan. You see, in my work as a private investigator, I have to watch places that may have bad things going on. I was watching one of those places when I say this person that may be involved in criminal activity. I never saw him again, and I wanted more information on him, so I had an artist draw this from what I remembered about how he looked," Sidney told him.

"I get it. He's the bad guy."

"Yes, at least I think so. I'll need to do more investigating, but yes I think he is a bad guy."

Ryan reached across the table picking up the paper and looked hard at the drawing.

"What are you doing?" Sidney inquire seeing the look on Ryan's face.

"I'm investigating," Ryan answered quite seriously.

Sidney smiled at the thought of his four-old-son mimicking his father. He wasn't sure he wanted him to follow in his footsteps one PI in the family was bad enough especially with Leslie always getting involved. He bowed his head and thanked the Lord for his son and asked protection for both him, his mother Lesley and himself. Amen. He said out loud.

"Dad, did you pray in your head," Ryan said.

"Yes, Son."

Then with his head bowed Ryan said, "Amen."

*****

Several days passed and Sidney was still staked out at the French Market. He was making some progress but was discouraged by the time involved. He wanted to spend more time with his family, and he knew Leslie wanted him home more. One day as he straightened the scarves on the table once again. He saw, out of the corner of his eye, the same guy he had seen a few weeks ago. He maneuvered around the table to get a better look. Yep, it was the same guy. He was amazed at the resemblance to the artist sketch. This guy had tattoos up and down both muscular arms bulging beneath a sleeveless t-shirt. His black hair was pulled back in a ponytail and matched his unkempt beard. He seemed upset about something and was talking loudly at the old man behind the counter. All Sidney could make out was he couldn't get the merchandise right now but would try later when the coast was clear. Once, he looked Sidney's way but quickly looked back at the old man. It wasn't long until he left. Sidney wanted to follow him but thought better of it. Instead, he struck up a conversation with his vendor neighbor.

"Boy, he seemed really angry. I hope it wasn't anything you did. He's a big guy, and I would hate to meet him in the alley if you know what I mean," Sidney said.

"Oh, he gets that way every once in a while. I just listen to him blow off steam, and he gets over it," the old man said sitting back down on his stool.

"You two must do business together."

"Yeah, that's what he is upset about."

"Really?"

"Just a little misunderstanding. He'll get over it," the old man said wiping the sweat from his brow. "He thinks he has it bad in his job. He ought to try sitting here in the heat every day as we do. Right?"

"Right."

So they were doing business together and maybe this big guy was fencing his wares with the old man. The guy looked like a laborer of sorts, even had some paint on his work clothes. I wonder where he works, what does he do in his day job. We may now know what he does in his night job. Sidney thought working out the details in his mind.

Chapter **12**

It was a work day at the Bordeaux estate, and everyone was busy with their assignments. Rose Marie, the oldest sister, was helping Katrina Louise in the bedrooms upstairs, sorting their mother's things. Patrick, Rose Marie's husband, the one in the family with a green thumb, was on the grounds surrounding the house pulling weeds with Jonathon.

"Do you suppose A.J. will show up?" Jonathon said with glove-clad hands yanking on what was left of an ivy vine growing on the fence.

"Not much telling. She marches to her own drummer, so to speak, and I don't think she is into manual labor," Patrick remarked, knowing his sister-in-law.

"I'm so glad Katrina Louise included us on this project. I know she didn't have too. But it's a way for everyone to see some of the money lost in the trust. I get sick to my stomach every time I think about what I put the family through. It was never my intention to embezzle money from the family trust," Jonathon said, not looking at Patrick.

"Let's put that behind us, Jonathon. One thing is for sure, it brought you back to a closer relationship with the Lord. It may not seem like it was worth everything we all went through. However, I for one am grateful you called on God to be your friend and to give you his grace."

"Yeah, and he's still my friend. I talk to him every day. I thank him every day for the gift of his son and the forgiveness of my sins," Jonathon said wiping his brow with the back of the glove on his hand.

Just then A.J. came around the corner of the galley dressed in her usual provocative attire. Jonathon and Patrick exchanged looks as she waved.

"Hi fellows," she said. "I had things to do this morning. Getting kids off to school and things. I don't know how much help I can be, but here I am."

"Do you have any work gloves? These weeds can really cut your hands without protection," Patrick told her.

"I don't wear work gloves, and I don't pull weeds. Isn't there something else I can do that is not so hard? I'm not a man, isn't this man's work?" she said whining.

"You could drag these bags to the curb where the trash haulers could pick them up in the morning."

"Well, I guess I can try, but it's a long way from here to the curb. Don't we have a wagon or something to put these bags on?

"That's a good idea. Do you have a wagon we can use?" Jonathon said.

"No Jonathon. I don't have a wagon….you…," she stopped before she said something she'd regret to Jonathon. She still did not trust him, and she got mad every time she saw him because he stole her money.

"Come on Jonathon, let's go look in the storage shed in the back, maybe we can find something to carry the bags in," Patrick said knowing that things could get worse if A.J. continued.

When they came back to where they left A.J., she was nowhere in sight. Patrick looked around then through the large window in the parlor he saw her standing very close to the man Katrina Louise hired to do some work on the house. He noticed both of them exchanging touches, laughing and cutting up. From what Jeffrey had told him about this Nick character, he was not happy with the way his sister-in-law was acting. Leaving Jonathon behind, he headed toward the front door of the house. He entered the parlor where A.J. and Nick were.

"There you are. We found something to help with the bags," he said coming closer to the two of them. "Hello, my name is Patrick," he said offering his hand.

"Hi. I'm Nick," he said then backing away from A.J., much to her disappointment he said. "Who do you belong to? Or should I say who are you related too in this family?"

"I'm A.J.'s brother-in-law," Patrick said firmly. "Come on A.J. let the man work."

"Your little sister… in-law and I were getting acquainted," Nick said winking at A.J. to her delight.

"I saw that. However, we have work to do and so do you," Patrick said giving A.J. a look that made her turn and follow him outside.

"What's the matter, Patrick? You jealous?"

Patrick didn't justify the question with an answer instead handed her a pair of gloves then went back to pulling weeds. A.J. put the gloves on and tried to pick up a bag then drug it over to the wagon. Struggling she finally managed to load it in the wagon.

"One bag down and many more to go," Jonathon said watching as his sister pull the wagon down to the gate.

"I doubt she has ever done anything in the form of labor. This is really going to be hard for her. We probably should figure out something she can do other than physical labor," Patrick said.

"You're right. Let's have a talk with Katrina Louise later. Maybe she can work in the house with Rose Marie. I think she's sorting through mom and dad's things," Jonathon said with unexpected compassion toward his sister.

A.J. wiped the sweat from her brow and let out a few curse words. Then took the gloves off and declared she quit. Jonathon and Patrick continued working ignoring the complaining.

"Jonathon we wouldn't be in this mess if it wasn't for you. I don't think it's fair that we have to work to get the money back when it was you who lost all of our money."

"I'm sorry, Sis. I know this is hard for you and I don't blame you for being angry with me. Let's see if we can find something more comfortable for you to do," Jonathon said. "And A.J. please don't use that kind of language. It's not becoming for a lady to talk that way."

"Well, look who is calling the kettle black. You really have no room to talk about anything brother of mine. Not after what you did. Just because they didn't keep you in jail doesn't mean I don't know what you did," A.J. said stomping off toward the house.

Chapter **13**

Since the Bordeaux siblings were helping Katrina Louise, Leslie was excluded, but she was still working on finding out who Nick Nixon was and what he was doing in New Orleans. She searched the names of his friends in the boarding house but found no indication that they knew him before he arrived in New Orleans. Assuming Nick was short for Nickolas, she changed her tactics and began searching for a Nickolas. That brought some luck.

There were several names listed but not in Louisianna let alone New Orleans. So she began to search for each name to find their occupation. It wasn't long until she was able to identify four Nickolas' in the construction business. She ran their names through the public records and through criminal records. Her search led to a Nickolas who worked on a ship at one time that docked in New Orleans. This was the first lead she had found, and she became convinced it was the same Nick Nixon. He was listed as a mechanic and had worked on the ship for several years. His mailing address was listed in Breaux Bridge, Louisianna.

*****

Sidney missed the time spent with Leslie. He yearned for the days past when they spent romantic get-aways on the weekends. Determined to make it up to her, he arranged for the other agent to cover for him at the French Market for a few days. He called and asked Daisy, the nanny, if she could stay with Ryan, and she agreed. He asked her not to say anything to Leslie.

"Hello, Mrs. Rye. How has your day been," Sidney said coming up behind her in the kitchen and kissing her on the cheek. He then turned around and patted Ryan on the top of his head, then messing with his hair, he said, "And have you been a good boy today?"

"Yes, he has. Daisy left early today, so Ryan and I've spent the afternoon together. We went to the park and the grocery store, and now he's helping me fix dinner," she said with pride.

"Well, he's doing a good job of snapping those green beans," Sidney said heading upstairs to change clothes before dinner.

Coming back downstairs, he watched as Ryan helped his mother set the table. Sidney had not been home to share dinner with his family for a while, and he looked forward to the three of them sitting down together. Sidney asked the blessing on their food, and all three said amen.

"Dad, are you still investigating?" Ryan said with a mouth full of green beans.

"Don't talk with your mouth full, Ryan," Leslie scolded.

"Yes Son, but I'm going to take some time off and take your mom on a little trip," Sidney said smiling at Leslie.

"Where are you going?"

"We haven't decided yet. I think I'll leave that up to your mom."

"Why?" Ryan asked.

"Because…" then he looked at Ryan and laughed knowing that no matter what his answer Ryan would ask why.

After dinner, they cleaned up the kitchen and sent Ryan off to bath and get ready for bed. They sat at the table drinking decaf coffee.

"So, any ideas of where you would like to spend a few days with me," Sidney said. "and don't worry about Ryan. I have already made arrangements with Daisy."

"I'm excited, surprised and wondering what brought this on," she said grinning.

"I miss you."

"I miss you too."

"So, where should we go?"

"Beaux Bridge," she said without hesitation.

"Really?" he said confused.

"Don't get mad, but I found some information on Nick, and it leads to Beaux Bridge."

"I see. Not the romantic time I was looking for, however knowing you, we better follow your instincts," Sidney said with a sigh.

"It'll still be romantic. I just want to check out a couple of things and the rest of the time is ours. Okay?"

"Sure, no problem," he said knowing when she set her head on something there was no changing her mind.

A few days later, with many hugs, and be a good boy to Ryan, they headed to the tiny town of Beaux Bridge known for it's Crawfish Festival in the spring. Taking Highway 10 towards Lafayette reminded them of another time Leslie and Annabelle found themselves in trouble on that same highway. She and Sidney laughed about it as they drove along reminiscing. It was about one hundred thirty miles to their destination, but they were in no hurry and decided to stop in Baton Rouge the capital of Louisianna and second largest city in the state and do some site seeing. Sidney wanted to see the old Arsenal Museum. Lesley took a picture of Sidney standing and looking out over the land. She was reminded of what a handsome husband she married. She enjoyed the beauty of the grounds surrounding the museum and Sidney took a picture of her beside some native flowers in bloom.

It was getting late in the day, and they drove on to Beaux Bridge and checked into a motel then walked down the main street and stopped at a café advertising the best crawfish étouffée in Louisianna. Coming from New Orleans, they found that hard to believe but were pleasantly surprised or maybe it was because they were so hungry.

The next morning Leslie wanted to see if she could find out anything about Nick, so she started with the phone book thinking perhaps he had relatives in the area. Little did she know that the phone book listed its townspeople by their nicknames. She couldn't believe her eyes. Most of the names, in some way, indicated what they were known for, or how people perceived them. The French Cajans had a real sense of humor, and it showed in the names in this little book. Names like Bayou Beaux or Crawfish Mamma were throughout the book. Since it was a small town and everyone knew everyone or somebody that did, she decided that she and Sidney would start asking the locals if they knew anyone that knew a Nick Nixon.

"Hi, I use to know a guy named Nickolos Nixon that lived here. Would you happen to know if he still lives here or if he has relatives that live here?" Leslie asked the clerk at the motel where they were staying.

"No. But I've only lived here for two years. Some of the old-timers might know," he answered.

"Thanks, I'll ask around," Leslie said leaving with Sidney.

"This could be a wild goose chase, you know," he told her.

"True, but worth a try, right?"

They ate a breakfast of pain perdu (French toast). Then they talked to everyone in the café. After breakfast, they walked up and down the main drag with Leslie stopping people on the street. She especially targeted the older folks hoping they would remember old Nick, the sea waring mechanic that had a post office box in their little town in Louisianna.   Sidney finally got in the swing of things and sat down beside a salty old fellow right out of the swamps.

"Nice day."

"Yep, dey 'gators wel be out fo' sho'," he said.

"Say, would you happen to know a fellow by the name of Nickolos Nixon?" Sidney asked.

The old man sat chewing on something, Sidney was not quite sure what was hanging from his lips. Looking down at the crack in the sidewalk he said slowly,

"Sho' nouf, w'at ya wan' of him,"

"I use to know him on the ship and just wondered how he was doing, just catching up," Sidney said.

"Dat yo' woman?"

"Yeah, she's been helping me look for him," Sidney said knowing he was suspicious.

His face was rough with deep wrinkles, eyes deep in their sockets, teeth were rotten and missing, and he smelled of fish. Sidney surmised that he could be in his fifties, but he looked seventy. His fingers were snarled and twisty making it hard for him to remove the thing in his mouth. He looked straight at Sidney with anger on his face.

"De mony t'is manh o' ye?"

"No. Does he owe you money?"

"Dat he do, de snak' belly," the old fellow said.

"Is he from around here?"

"On de bay-ou," he said waving toward the swampland.

"Well, if I catch up with him I'll let you know. Thanks for the talk."

Sidney caught up with Leslie and gave her the information from the old guy. He felt sorry for him and wondered why Nick owed him money. Now that they knew he was from around here they were determined to find out more. The bloodhound in Leslie made Sidney glad he was with her, and she hadn't gone out on her own following this lead. They decided to get closer to where the swamp people lived and made their living with tours through the bayou under the moss hanging from the live oaks and cypress trees. It was close to noon now so after lunch they would see about getting on a tour.

The swamps of Lake Martin filled their ears with the sounds of frogs, spoonbills and tail splashing alligators swooping passed them skillfully gliding toward the shore. Egrets filled the branches of the bald cypress trees rising from the deep murky water. Their nostrils took in the indescribable smells only found in the swamplands. Sudden noises turned their heads in anticipation. It was hot and humid as the sun peeked through the trees exposing the brown colored water surrounding the boat. Suddenly zydeco music was heard in the distance, and they knew they would soon pull into shore for a little shopping for souvenirs.

Sidney helped Leslie from the boat, and as they looked over the wares offered by the Cajuns, they asked questions. However, it was not something the people wanted or would talk about. Soon frustration set in and Leslie stepped outside on the wooden deck surrounding the building and bowing her head she prayed. *Father, thank you for my wonderful patient husband. Sometimes I feel I don't deserve him. All he wanted was a romantic time with me, and here I am dragging him to who knows where trying to get information on this Nick character. Lord, if this is the place I should be, and if I'm supposed to discover something here, please, if it's Your will, show me the way. I feel I have been led to this place. I'm in your hands, God. Oh, Holy Spirit, guide me. In Jesus' Name. Amen.*

Before re-boarding the boat they saw an unbelievable sunset through the trees as shades of pinks and purples covered the horizon. Darkness began to blanket the swamp and the sounds from the frogs and species of night birds were deafening. With the lights from the boat leading the way, alligator eyes peered out from the water around them as they made their way back to Beaux Bridge. The heat from the day gave way to a chill over the water. Sidney put his arm around Leslie's shoulders drawing her close to him to keep her warm. Not a word was spoken as the experienced guide weaved in and out among the cypress trees. When the water narrowed, the swamp sounds increased, warning them of the shores closing in on them. Once in while, a gasp permeated the air as an unidentified insect flew into someone's face. Soon the lights from the town were visible.

Back at the motel, Leslie and Sidney took a shower hoping to remove the musty smells from their bodies. They put on fresh clothes and set out to find another place to eat dinner. Both tired from a long day, they ate in silence.

"T'is manh Nick yo'w'nt to no' 'bout?" a firm-statured, round-faced woman suddenly standing next to them, asked with great authority.

"Yes," Sidney said wiping his mouth of food residue. "Here sit with us. Do you have information for us?"

"De bay-ou I no t'ings. T'is manh about y' wan'. Work' on a s'ip in de wa'er fix t'ings de s'ip t'is true?" the woman said sitting in a chair at the edge of the table.

"Yes," Leslie said leaning forward to better understand the woman's Cajun dialect.

All she could make out was that he was a gambler and lost money to a lot of Cajuns living on the bayou. It was also thought he might have killed someone in the swamps and then disappeared.

"How long ago was that?" Leslie asked interested since his time in New Orleans only went back two years.

"y'rs go' t'irty," the woman said looking deep into Leslie's eyes giving her a chill.

They thanked the woman as she left refusing their offer of a meal. Looking at each other both in their own thoughts as they processed this information. *So where has he been all this time? What has he been up to over the thirty or so years since anyone around here knew of him? Who did he supposedly kill?* These questions rolled around in Leslie's head. Then out loud she said to Sidney.

"We need more information. Can you use your PI influence at the police station and find out if he was ever charged with a crime because when I checked the records, his name didn't show up."

"On one condition, we don't do anything about this until morning. We don't even talk about it. Okay?" Sidney said pleading with her.

"Okay, you're right. Let's go down the street to that place where they dance. We haven't been dancing in a long time," Leslie said.

"Did we ever go dancing?" he said confused.

"Oh, Sid. Of Course, we went dancing…didn't we?" she said shaking her head in despair.

"Well, if we did your memory is better than mine. Anyway, let's do it."

Zydeco music from a band of unusual instruments of washboards, juice-harps, wash-tub fiddles and squeeze boxes lured them further down the street where they found the open aired building shaking from the stomping feet keeping time with the music. Lesley felt a connection to the people in this little town that filled her soul. Thoughts of her mom and the father of whom she had never known, both Louisianna natives, as far as she knew, brought a smile to her face as Sidney took her hand and pulling her on the dance floor with all the others began to swirl her around holding her by the waist. She squealed when he pushed her away then brought her back so close to him she could feel him breathing. For the first time in a long time, they were kids again without a care in the world. *Thank you father, thank you for putting Sidney in my life. I'm so ever grateful for this wonderful man, my husband*

and the father of my child. She prayed when Sidney went to get them something to drink. Coming back to the table, he handed her a glass of lemonade with ice and a straw.

"Now this is fun, and this is what I wanted us to do when I came up with this plan," Sidney said giving her a wink.

"Thank you. I love you, Sid."

The next morning, as promised, Sidney went to the local police department. Flashing his license, he handed over his business card and asked the desk clerk if he could talk to someone about a missing person. Just then a salty looking character came through the open door of an office presumably belonging to the police chief. He stood, in his uniform long overdue of ironing, next to Sidney and inquired about the missing person Sidney was referring to.

"His name is Nickolos Nixon, and I understand at one time he lived here on the bayou. My information came from someone who knew of him say thirty years ago. Supposedly he was a gambler and may have killed someone," Sidney said matter-a-factly.

"Well sir, the bayou is full of stories. Some true others made up to satisfy the audience. I hear you and the lady…," He began.

"My wife," Sidney interrupted.

"Your wife… have been asking questions. This is a small town where word gets around fast. The bayou person you spoke to? What did she tell you that made you believe her?"

"It was more the fact that she looked for us and didn't want anything in return," Sidney told him.

"Yes… that would make things a little more believable." Turning, he motioned for Sidney to follow him into his office.

They both sat down across from each other on either side of a large military desk. The chief took out a blank pad and reached across to retrieve a pen. Looking at Sidney, he began to ask questions. It was soon established that the missing person might not be missing at all. This intrigued the police chief, and he told Sidney that if this man were in their cold case file, he would let him know. After shaking hands, Sidney left the office, nodded at the desk clerk and headed for the door. He heard the police chief ask the desk clerk to bring him the files on unsolved cases going back thirty years. Then Sidney went through the door and outside where Leslie was waiting.

"Well, anything?"

"The police chief seemed very interested, and since it had been thirty years since Nick was heard from on the bayou, he is checking the cold case files. Hard copies it looks like, and he said he would call me if he found anything."

"Well, that's a start. Did you tell him he was a gambler?" Leslie said as they walked hand in hand back down the main street.

"Yeah, and that he may have killed someone. At first, he was telling me that the bayou people don't always tell the truth. However after I told him the person giving us the information didn't want anything in return, he changed his attitude. So this may lead us somewhere," he said.

Leslie waited until Sidney could be with her to call Ryan. She dialed the number, and when Daisy answered, she handed the phone to Ryan.

"Hello son, are you being a good boy for Daisy?"

"Yes, I'm investigating," he said.

"That's good son," Sidney and Leslie smiled at each other. "Where are you doing your investigating?"

"In my room," Ryan said with pride.

"We will be home tomorrow. We love you, Ryan, ask Daisy if she needs to talk to us? Goodbye, see you tomorrow,"

Daisy told them that Ryan was being good and played in his room most of the time, but they had gone to the park twice, and Miss Annabelle came to see him. They thanked Daisy and hung up. Missing their little boy, they were anxious to return to New Orleans. The rest of the day found them sightseeing as they waited to hear from the police chief about the cold cases. As they sat down for dinner, Sidney's cell phone rang.

"Hello."

"Mr. Rye?" Chief Billy, as he was known to the townspeople, said.

"Yes."

"We're still going through several boxes of files. I just didn't want you to think we weren't on top of this. Will you be around for a while?"

"Actually we plan to leave first thing in the morning. However, I would appreciate it if when you find something you give me a call. If we need to come back that won't be no problem," Sidney looked at Leslie, and she nodded in agreement.

"Okay, then we'll keep digging, and hopefully we find something."

"Thank you. We'll keep in touch."

Chapter **14**

"So you really think this is the same guy," Annabelle said with her phone to her ear.

"It sure looks like it could be," Leslie said.

"If he murdered someone, why would he still use his given name?" Annabelle questioned.

"You know, Sidney and I talked about that on the way home from Beaux Bridge. That murder thing could be rumors. If he owed people money from gambling, those same people would want him in trouble and make up that story. But on the other hand, the story could be factual, but he knows no one can prove it. What if the person he killed was dumped in the swamp? No one would be able to find the body what with all the creatures in the swamp."

"Do you mean like alligators?"

"Yeah, unless they killed the alligator and found a body," Leslie said shaking from the thought.

"Oh Leslie, you and your imagination," Annabelle laughed at her friend's explanation of events. "I guess it could happen, but that is not a sure thing for him to count on in any scenario."

"I tell you what, that swamp tour was something nightmares are made from, especially coming back at night. It was very scary. I was so glad Sidney was beside me," Leslie told her.

"For some reason, I can't think of you being afraid of anything. Not my comrade who takes chances at the drop of a hat."

"You weren't there, Annabelle, with all the moss hanging from the cypress trees and the swampy brown water full of snakes and alligators. My skin crawls just thinking about it," Leslie said.

"Now you're making me squirm. Let's talk about something else. Jeffrey and I are working on our wedding plans. We have decided on a date… May 10th. I hope that works for you since I want you to be my matron of honor."

"Wow, that's not far away. Are you sure you can get it together by then? And I'll be glad to help in any way I can, as your friend and your matron of honor," Leslie said jotting the memo on her calendar.

"Oh, thank you, Leslie. Let's get together soon and go over some things," Annabelle said dispelling her anxiety. I better get back to work. I'll check with you later on a time and place."

Sidney was back at work at the French Market. He noticed the old man filling boxes with merchandise. "You're not going to move, are you? I thought you were doing a good deal of business in this location."

"Something has come up with my partner. We're going to shut it down for now and maybe move further north while the weather is so hot and humid here. Anyway, it has been interesting working next to you. Your buddy didn't talk to me as much, and I must say I missed you. Did you have a good vacation with your wife in Beaux Bridge?"

"Yes, we did. I don't remember telling you about our vacation plans," Sidney said.

"Your buddy told me you went to Beaux Bridge. Not the most romantic place in the world if you were trying to impress your wife," the old man said continuing to pack.

Sidney thought for a moment *that he hadn't told Charles where they were going. So how did this old man know where they went. He had better warn Leslie.* Excusing himself, he left the area and called Leslie.

"I don't understand. Why would anyone want to know where we went and how did they find out?" Leslie said confused.

"I don't like this Les, this guy that I've been looking for could be the very person that knew where we were going. The puzzle is that no-one knew until after we left. Daisy wouldn't tell anyone," Sidney said trying to figure it out.

"Even if she did tell someone, Sid, who would have wanted to know where we were going and why?"

"Wait a minute, could someone in Beaux Bridge have informed this guy that we were in Beaux Bridge. Could it be this Nick character is the jewelry guy's partner? That would make sense because we talked to everyone and his brother while in Beaux Bridge."

"But you said he hadn't been back to the Market. Do you really think it could be Nick?" Leslie said trying to follow Sidney's line of thought.

"Well, if it's Nick and he suddenly decides to leave town we will know it's him. In the meantime be careful and Leslie, don't go over to the Bordeaux House. Understood?"

"You know me too well Sidney Rye. But I promise I won't go over there. But shouldn't we warn Annabelle?"

"The fewer people know about this, the better. I'll put Charles on surveillance at the Bordeaux House, and you keep all doors locked and stay inside, okay?"

"Okay," Leslie said. "What are you going to do?"

"I think I'll see about getting a room at the boarding house. What was it called?"

"The Bayou Manor, wait a minute, I have the phone number and address right here," Leslie said. "Are you going to stay there? The owner is really talkative full of information if you just listen she will tell you more than you want to know. Be careful Sid. I love you."

So as to not draw suspicion, Sidney told the old man that he had an emergency at home but would be back in a couple of hours. It occurred to him that Charles may have seen Nick come into the market while he and Leslie were gone. He called Charles on his way to the car. After their conversation, he was convinced that Charles had not seen the guy in the artist rendition so assigned him to the Bordeaux House and he headed for the Bayou Manor.

Making sure Nick's red truck wasn't parked outside, he went through the door into the desk at the front and waited for the owner to answer the bell over the door. A friendly woman with a big smile came through the opening behind the desk.

"Yes, may I help you?"

"I noticed the no vacancy sign outside but was wondering if there will be an opening coming up soon? With hotel bills so high I'd rather stay here. I'm interested in maybe two or three nights," Sidney said.

"Well, sir we don't have much of a turnover. Most of the people staying here have full-time jobs, and they call this home. We have three guys that ride together to their jobs, and they all get along so well… Pardon me," she said as she answered the phone on the desk. "Hello. Yes, sergeant, I did call, thank you for getting back with me. At first, I thought I had just misplaced my rings, you know took them off somewhere and didn't remember where I put them. I'm a little forgetful. But I have looked everywhere, and I can't find them. Do you suppose someone took them?"

Sidney pretended to look around and not listen while the woman talked in a low voice with her back turned to him,

"I see. Well they were or I should say are very expensive. My husband bought them for me many years ago. I haven't had them appraised lately, but twelve years ago they were worth thousands of dollars," She listened then said. "I did call my insurance company, and they said they would have to have a police report. So that's why I called you."

Soon the conversation ended, and she turned back around and called to Sidney who had picked up a newspaper and was looking through the want ads. He turned around and walked back to the desk. "I guess I better find another place. Do you know of any around here? This area is so convenient that I'd like to stay close."

"I'm sorry. If you leave a number, I could let you know if I have a vacancy any time soon," She said.

"I appreciate that but unless one comes up in a day or two… well, I guess I'll just look somewhere else. Thank you for your time," Sidney said walking out the door.

Back in his car, he started to back out of his parking space when he saw a red pickup truck pull in to a parking space on the side of the manor where the residents parked. He waited, then pulled away after the man went into the house. Sidney found a place close by that gave him a view of the front and the back of the manor. He called Charles and was told that Nick had left the Bordeaux House. Sidney told Charles to head for his own house and keep an eye on Leslie and Ryan.

Soon Sidney watched as the man came out of the Manor and threw his suitcase in the back seat of his truck. Sidney made a note of the make of the truck, a red F150 Ford extended cab. When he pulled out of his parking place, Sidney followed. It was late in the day and traffic was picking up. Sidney kept the red truck in his view as he realized they were headed to the Garden District. He took in a deep breath as the pick up turned to head for his own house. Preparing himself for what was ahead he was surprised when the truck kept going. Then he realized he and the red truck were headed for the Bordeaux House. He now knew it was Nick and he slowed down and parked as he watched Nick pull up next to the curb by the front gate. Sidney couldn't believe his eyes as he watched A.J. run out from behind the house and jump in the passenger side and slide in beside Nick.

When Nick pulled away from the curb, Sidney followed staying a distance but keeping him in sight. The after-work traffic made it hard to stay up with the red truck, and soon Sidney lost sight of it. *He is probably headed to the market.* Sidney thought. So taking his cell phone and making sure Charlie was still at his post, he headed for the Market in the French Quarter. He went a different direction but ran into a traffic jam due to an accident in an intersection. Trying to turn around was next to impossible on the tight two-lane road. He was growing impatient when suddenly the police opened the other lane for one-way traffic. He went around the accident and made his way to the Market. Just as he pulled in behind the market, he saw the red pickup with empty glass jewelry cases and boxes filling the back of the truck leave the parking area. Following close behind was a panel van with the old man at the wheel. Sidney was pointed in the wrong direction to get in behind them. Once again he had to turn his vehicle around. He watched helplessly as the truck and van headed back into the French Quarter. Try as he may, he couldn't catch up with them. Frustrated at losing them he remembered A.J. was with Nick. He called Leslie. After telling her what was going on, he asked her to see if she could find out where A.J. lived without causing any suspicions.

Finally, the phone rang. "Hello, Les?"

"I can't get ahold of anyone. Annabelle is not answering her phone, and neither is Jeffrey. They must be talking to each other, and that's why they aren't answering even though they probably know it's me. I guess they figure they'll call back after they get through talking," Leslie told Sidney.

"Great, what about Rose Marie. Did you try her?"

"Same thing. What should I do?" Leslie asked knowing how frustrated Sidney sounded.

"Call Katrina Louise."

"She will want an explanation for sure."

"Give her one. Tell her you are helping Annabelle with a list for wedding invitations."

"Super. I'll call you back."

The phone rang several times as Leslie began to pray. *Father, please let me get through to someone for A.J.'s sake.* A voice answered giving Leslie a fright.

"Katrina Louise, is that you?"

"Yes. Who is this?"

"It's Leslie," she said trying not to sound as anxious as she felt. "Did I interrupt something, you sound out of breath."

"No. I was outside talking to Jonathon. I left my cell in the kitchen," she said.

"I'm compiling a list for Annabelle for wedding invitations. Could you give me A.J.'s address?" she said calmly.

"I don't know if I have her new address. She moves so often. I have her cell number if you want to call her," Katrina Louise said.

"I hate to bother her. Would you mind checking to see if you might have it in your contact list?"

"Sure, hold on a minute," She said looking in her contacts. "Okay, I think this is her latest address. You may want to check it."

"Thank you, Katrina Louise," Leslie said.

"Sure. Did you and Sidney enjoy your little trip?" She asked.

"Yes. Oh, I'm sorry that's Sidney on the other line. Thanks again," She lied to get off the phone so that she could call him back.

She hung up and dialed Sidney. Telling him it may not be A.J.'s latest address, didn't help the situation any as he reminded her to keep the doors locked and not to leave the house. He told her Charlie was still watching the house but not to take any chances. She assured him she would do as he said and hung up. Bowing her head, she prayed. *Heavenly Father, thank you for being with us. Help Sidney find A.J. before something happens to her. Keep them safe, Lord. Oh, Father please keep A.J.'s children safe and out of harm's way. If Nick has her against her will, give her courage and strength to get herself out of the situation. This I pray in Jesus' Name. Amen.*

The ringing of her phone startled her. She didn't realize how stressed she was. Then looking at the phone, she saw it was Annabelle.

"Hello."

"Hi. I saw where you called. What can I do for you?

"I just wondered if you were making a list for invitations. I've started one, and you can edit it later. I didn't know A.J.'s address, and I just thought you or Jeffrey might know it."

"Well, miss efficiency. Let me look. Yes, here it is. But Leslie this may be an old address. I think she may have moved since this one. I can check with Jeffrey and give you a callback."

"Okay, if you don't mind," Leslie said worried that Annabelle could tell something was wrong by the sound of her voice.

She called Sidney and told him that Annabelle was checking with Jeffrey on the latest address. Then she asked Sidney if she could tell Annabelle. "She'll keep it quiet until we find out what is going on and I'm afraid her radar will be out anyway. I just can't keep things from her, Sid."

"Please wait, Les. I have just turned on the street where A.J. may live, and I don't see any sign of the truck or the van."

"Any sign of the kids," she said almost in a whisper.

"No. I'll sit here until I hear from you, okay?"

When Annabelle called back, she gave Lesley the same address that Katrina Louise had provided her and Jeffrey was sure that was the latest known address for A.J. She thanked Annabelle and told her she had to get Ryan ready for bed and would talk to her later. That seemed to satisfy her, and they hung up. Leslie let Sidney know and told him their secret was still safe.

It was dark now, and Sidney was still parked down the street from A.J.'s house. He saw a car pull into the driveway and watched as the three children got out of the car and went into the house. The lights went on, and soon the oldest boy came back out to the car and unloaded what looked like grocery bags. Another boy came out and helped. With the car locked up, they took the bags in the house and shut the front door. Sidney could see in the kitchen window and watched as the three children unloaded the bags putting things away. Then the boys left the room, and the girl stayed in the kitchen.

Sitting in his car watching A.J.'s children basically taking care of themselves, made his heart ache. *Where was A.J.? What kind of mess was she in? Did she go willingly?* He wasn't sure how he felt at this point. He waited another couple of hours thinking they may have gone somewhere to unload. He reviewed everything he knew to this point. *But they could be out of the state by now. The old man had said they were going up north. If he was still with the FBI, he would have an APB out on them all ready. Maybe he should tell Annabelle. She knows people in the DA's office.*

When Sidney got home, Leslie heated his dinner and while he ate she began to ask questions. But he didn't have any answers. He told her about A.J.'s children and how they appeared to be used to her not being around. She asked if he thought she told them she was leaving and that is why they went to the store.

"Maybe A.J. and Nick went by the house before you got there. Maybe you should talk to the kids tomorrow and see what they know." Just then Ryan came down the stairs.

"Hi, Buddy, what are you doing out of bed?" Sidney said lifting his son up on his lap.

"Have you been investigating, Dad?"

"Yes, son. I have, that's why I'm so late."

"Dad?"

"Yes, Son."

"You know that picture of the bad guy?"

"Yes," Sidney said putting some food in his mouth.

"I saw him. You know the bad guy in the picture."

Sidney swallowed hard and clearing his throat asked Ryan where he saw the bad guy.

"When you and mom were gone I saw him go inside my playhouse."

'Where were you, Ryan?"

"In my room looking out the window. I can see my playhouse from my window. You know, Mom. I told you that."

Leslie looked at Sidney with fear on her face. Sidney put his fork down and looked at Ryan.

"So you like investigating, don't you. Like, Dad?"

"Yes, can I have a piece of your cake?"

"In a minute. Where was Daisy when you were investigating and saw the bad guy?"

"I guess she was asleep," Ryan said keeping an eye on the chocolate cake.

"So it was night time. Was it dark outside?"

"Not yet, I was supposed to be asleep, but sometimes I look out my window to see if I can see the moon yet," Ryan said squirming.

Leslie looked at Ryan and saw him focused on the cake. She brought the plate close to her and sliced the piece of square cake in half. She moved part of the cake onto Sidney's now empty plate and set the smaller plate in front of Ryan.

"Thanks, mom," Ryan said taking Sidney's clean spoon and putting a piece of cake to his mouth getting chocolate icing all over his lips and chin.

Wiping his mouth with a napkin, Leslie asked Ryan how he could see the bad man in the dark. Waiting for him to put another bite in his mouth, she asked again. He looked at her with a puzzled look and told her, "It wasn't dark yet, mom. So, I know it was him."

Sidney reached down and opened his briefcase. He pulled out the picture Ryan had seen, and showed it to him again.

"Yes, that's him, Dad. The lights in the playhouse were on, and he went in and talked to the man building my playhouse."

"Son, you know that isn't your playhouse. It's mom's studio to write her books."

"I know, Dad. I'm just thinking in my head. You know, Dad, I wish it was my playhouse, so I pretend."

"Ryan, this is really important. Were you pretending you were investigating when you saw the bad man?"

Ryan thought a minute. Then with tears in his eyes, he looked at Sidney and told him he was not pretending.

"I saw him, Dad. It was him. Just like the picture."

"It's okay Ryan. I believe you. Now let's get you cleaned up, and mom and I'll put you back to bed. Let's you and I spend some time together in the morning. Okay, Buddy?"

"Okay, Dad," Ryan said wiping the tears from his face and jumping down from Sidney's lap.

Lesley cleaned Ryan's face and hands, and together they went upstairs and tucked Ryan in his bed making sure he would soon be asleep.

As they were about to leave the room, Ryan asked why would the bad guy be in his playhouse.

"I don't know for sure, Son. Don't worry about it. He was probably just looking at what a great playhouse it would make."

Back downstairs, they began to clear the table and clean up the kitchen all the time not saying anything. Sidney poured them another cup of decaf-coffee, and they went back to the dining room and sat at the table. Sidney pulled out a notepad and began to make notes.

"You believe him don't you?"

"I do, but there are so many things that don't add up. I think we need to get Jeffrey and Annabelle involved."

"The sooner, the better. I'll call Annabelle," she said, picking up her cell phone and pushing Annabelle's number.

Chapter **15**

Rose Marie invited her brother Jeffrey and Annabelle to their house for dinner. When they arrived, Patrick showed them to the kitchen where Rose Marie was putting the finishing touches on the meal. Jeffrey went outside with Patrick to retrieve the pork ribs from the grill.

"This is a real cozy kitchen Rose Marie I bet you and Patrick have had a lot of meals around this table in front of that bay window," Annabelle said walking over to the windows where she could see Jeffrey and Patrick on the patio.

"Where are you and Jeffrey going to live when you get married?"

"We haven't talked about that yet. I guess we have the cart before the horse. We're working on the wedding and honeymoon plans. I guess we haven't thought much about where we will live when we get back," Annabelle said helping Rose Marie set the table.

"Oh, Annabelle let me see your ring. It's quite beautiful."

Patrick and Jeffrey walked back in the kitchen with the ribs and set the pan on the stove.

"Jeffrey, where did you get Annabelle's ring?"

"We found it at the French Market. Do you like it?"

"It looks just like Mother's ring. In fact, I'm sure it is her ring. How on earth did it end up in the French Market?" Rose Marie asked holding Annabelle's hand and moving the ring around the finger.

"Are you sure?" Jeffrey asked.

"Well, if it's not hers, it's an exact copy," Rose Marie said. "I don't like what I'm thinking right now. Could it be part of Jonathon's embezzlement? Like maybe he sold it, and somehow it ended up at the French Market. Or maybe Margaret took it. She stopped talking then turning to Annabelle she told her she was sorry about everything she said and asked everyone to sit down. All through dinner her mind went back to the months during the trial hearing that Margaret, Jonathon's partner in crime had killed her husband and blackmailed Jonathon. Just thinking about Margaret being in her folk's home made her sick to her stomach.

"Father we come to you in celebration of Jeffrey and Annabelle's coming marriage. We ask your blessing on their marriage and their future together. Thank you, Jesus, for the many blessing you bestow on us daily and forgive us our transgressions. Bless the food for the nourishment of our bodies. In Your Name, Amen, " Patrick said as they each held hands around the table.

"Thank you, Patrick. Everything looks very tasty Rose Marie," Jeffrey said.

There was little conversation after the recognition of the ring. Each one was in their own thoughts as they enjoyed the meal. Every once in a while Jeffrey would catch Annabelle's eye and smiling he would give her a wink.

"I guess you are wondering how I know the ring so well. When mother was dying, she asked me to put the ring in safe keeping for her. There was a console table in the hall upstairs that had a hidden compartment in the back of the drawer. That's where she wanted me to put the ring. I took it off her finger and put it there as she asked. I hadn't thought about that until I saw the ring on Annabelle's finger. I had always admired Mother's ring, but I really examined it when I put it in that console."

"Is the console table still in the house?" Annabelle said.

"Yes, right where it has always been," Rose Marie stated.

"Did anyone else know about the hidden compartment?"

"I don't think so. I never knew about it, did you Jeffrey?" she said looking at him.

"No. I didn't know that and to be honest I never paid much attention to the table in the hall. It has always been there as a fixture in the house." Jeffrey told her.

"Well, we can't solve this mystery tonight so let's change the subject and have dessert. How does that sound?" Patrick said trying to change the mood.

After they enjoyed dessert and a fresh cup of coffee, they helped clear the table then said their goodbyes. As they headed to the door Annabelle's cell rang. Looking at the phone, she told Jeffrey it was Leslie.

"Hello."

"Annabelle, where are you?"

"We're just leaving Rose Marie's why?"

"Could you and Jeffrey come by on your way? We've something important to tell you both."

"Sure see you in a minute."

They drove a short distance to Sidney and Leslie's house. On the way, Annabelle shared her concern to Jeffrey that it could be about Ryan. Jeffrey calmed her saying, whatever it was they wanted to talk to them about, that God was in control and it would be alright.

Annabelle and Jeffrey walked up to the door and rang the doorbell. When Leslie opened the door, Annabelle knew something was wrong.

"What is it? Is Ryan okay?"

"Come on in. We're all fine, but we've something to tell you."

They came in and went to the dining room where all the essential meetings seemed to take place. Sitting down at the table they looked at Leslie and Sidney then asked again.

"What is it?"

"Let's start with the fact that someone told Nick that Les and I were in Beaux Bridge this past weekend. The jewelry booth I've had under surveillance has suddenly closed up shop." Sidney said.

"The same jewelry booth where we bought the ring?" Jeffrey said to Annabelle because he had seen Sidney there the day he was at the market and Sidney had told him he was on surveillance.

"No one knew where we were going that weekend we didn't know ourselves until the last minute. We called Daisy when we arrived and told her to call our cells if she needed us," Leslie said.

"So, when I found out the old man in the booth knew where we went I was sure it had something to do with Nick. This is the bad part. I put Charles at our house to watch Les and Ryan. I went to the Bayou Manor where Nick had a room and talked to the owner. She was talking to the police on the phone about her missing jewelry. I parked down the street and saw Nick come, park, go inside and come out with suitcases. I followed him all the way back to your folk's house, Jeffrey, where he pulled up to the curb, and I saw A.J. come out from behind the house and jump into the passenger side of his pickup."

Jeffrey sat quietly looking at Annabelle then back to Sidney.

"Are you saying she left town with him?"

"It appears that way. I followed them back to the market but got tied up in traffic, and I lost them after they loaded his pickup and a white panel truck. So, I headed for A.J.'s."

"That's why you wanted A.J.'s address," Annabelle said.

"Yes, but they never showed up or at least not while I was watching the place. I saw A.J.'s kids come home and unload groceries, so I don't know if they saw her before I got there or if she never went home."

"Did you talk to the kids?" Annabelle asked

"No. I told Sid I thought it best if someone in the family talked to them and ask some questions, you know to not scare them," Leslie said. "That's when we called you. And Annabelle, Ryan saw Nick out back in the studio while we were gone."

"What?" Annabelle said concerned.

Sidney told them about the artist rendition of the man he saw at the jewelry booth, and that was how Ryan knew it was Nick.

"Oh, this is scary. But why would he be out back? Where is A.J.? I had better call Rose Marie. She is close to A.J.'s kids. Maybe she can find out something," Jeffrey said taking out his cell and dialing the number.

After the call from Jeffrey, Rose Marie dialed A.J.'s number. There was no answer, so she and Patrick headed for A.J.'s house. On the way, Patrick told Rose Marie his observations concerning A.J. and Nick. He told her it sounded like she went willingly. Especially seeing how they acted around each other.

"Well, I wouldn't put it past her. But, what about the kids? Is Nick going to give her security or just a good time? Jeffrey said there/s more to the story than A.J. leaving with Nick. I don't know what he meant by that. I guess after we talk to the kids we ought to go over to Sidney and Leslie's and hear the whole story," Rose Marie said.

"Here we are, and it looks like the kids are still there. The lights are on, and Lance's car is here," Patrick said pulling in behind the car parked in the driveway. A.J.'s first born, now a handsome six foot 19 year old grew up fast taking care of his younger siblings while his mother negleted her children. Patrick did his best to give Lance advice and support. They had a lot of respect for each other.

They knocked on the door several times until A.J.'s oldest child, Lance, opened the door leaving the slide lock on. Seeing it was his Aunt and Uncle, he unlatched the lock and let them in. Beth and Tommy came running when they saw who it was and threw their arms around them. After a while, Patrick motioned to Lance to follow him into the kitchen leaving Rose Marie to stay with the other two children.

"What's wrong Uncle Patrick? Has something happened to Mom?" Lance said concerned.

"I've got a couple of questions. Did you see your mother anytime this evening?"

"Yes, she came by earlier and gave me some money for groceries and said she would be out of town for a few days and would let me know where to get in touch with her later," Lance told him.

"Was she with someone?" Patrick said.

"Some guy I didn't recognize. He stayed in the pick-up. What's going on?"

"We're not sure, Lance. The guy she left town with may be in some kind of trouble. We just want to make sure you kids are alright and then try to find your mother," Patrick said not wanting to scare him or his siblings. "Do you think she was happy to go with this guy?"

"Yeah, she was very excited. She ran up to her bedroom and came down with a suitcase. She kissed us all goodbye and left, after handing me the money. Said it was for food."

Satisfied with Lance's recollection of events Patrick went back in the other room with Lance following. He and Rose Marie said goodbye to the kids, Beth and Carl, assuring them they would be in touch and if they needed anything or heard from their mother to give them a call. Back in their car, Patrick related his conversation with Lance to Rose Marie.

"Well, at least she remembered to make sure the kids had food. That was kind of her," she said with great sarcasm. "Oh, I'm sorry that was an ugly thing to say. I should be praying she is safe. Let's go to the Ryes so they can tell us what's really going on."

Patrick didn't want to tell Rose Marie that Jeffrey had Leslie checking on Nick. Jeffrey had confided in Patrick one day at the house when Nick wasn't around. He was quite concerned for

Katrina Louise and was hoping, with the family helping, she could let Nick go, but it hadn't worked out that way. Patrick was also anxious to know what Leslie had discovered.

Sidney filled Rose Marie and Patrick in on the details and told them he would keep them up to date with any new information. Annabelle called her friend Bryce at the DA's office and told him about their suspicion concerning Nick. She asked Bryce if his office had any cause to be investigating Nick. He said he wasn't aware of any investigation but would see what he could find out. After everyone left Sidney made sure the house was secure, and he and Leslie went upstairs.

"This whole situation is strange, don't you think, Sid?" Leslie said from the bathroom as she prepared for bed.

"Very strange. I worry it could be dangerous too," he told her as she came out of the bathroom toward the bed.

"What was he doing out back with the men working on the studio? I wonder if he had been there before and I didn't notice?" Leslie said fluffing the pillows as she sat up next to Sidney and pulled the covers over her.

Sitting in bed, side by side, they both went silent as they contemplated their next move. "I asked Patrick to check with A.J.'s son, Lance, in the morning to see if he's heard from his mom and to let me know," Sidney said.

"Why on earth would she leave town with someone she hardly knows?"

"From what Patrick and Jeffrey told us tonight, it appears she wants a romantic involvement with Nick."

"But, Sid, she hasn't known him that long and what about her kid's. Is she that irresponsible? For all she knows he could be a very evil person taking advantage of her vulnerability," Leslie said rubbing her hands together with lotion and applying it to her arms and elbows. "What's the attraction? He must be in his sixties, and from my observation he's a womanizer, whatever that means?"

"Well, we can't solve this tonight, and it's late so let's get some sleep and work on this mystery in the morning," Sidney said kissing her forehead and turning out the lamp.

She reached over and switched off the lamp on her side of the bed. Taking Sidney's hand, she began to pray for A.J. and her children. *"Oh, Father, to you be the glory, you are our salvation, and your grace sustains us. Thank you, Father, for your protection and safekeeping of A.J. and Father keep our little boy safe from harm. In Jesus' Name. Amen."*

"Amen," Sidney said

Chapter **16**

Sitting in his apartment, Jonathon found himself depressed after days of working at the house he grew up in. So many things had happened since then. Graduations, marriages, births, illnesses, deaths, and trials. Yes, he must not forget his day in court. His heart still leaped out of his chest every time he thought about that part of his life. It was still hard to think about what he did to the family and now working beside them with one goal in mind to turn the house for a profit just brought everything to the surface. He appreciated the way Rose Marie and Patrick treated him as if nothing had happened. A.J. on the other hand really hated him and he didn't blame her. She couldn't even look him in the eye. He was glad when Katrina Louise found her something to do in the house.

Jonathon had always liked working with his hands. The major part of his business was repairing clocks. Now digging pulling weeds planting new vegetation and cleaning out the overgrowth had replaced his need to use his hands. He and Patrick worked well together on the grounds. They were making progress as they worked in sections. Once an area was finished they moved on to the next. Looking back at what they had accomplished inspired them to continue.

Patrick answered Jonathon's questions about the Bible, and he enjoyed their conversations about their faith. Jonathon had come a long way with his faith, and he knew without Jesus as his Savior he would be in a very bad place now. Anytime he felt down or unworthy he would begin to pray to acknowledge his gratitude to his Father in heaven and soon he was back on track. Many times since the trial he would experience great sorrow, and the pain would be unbearable. He would open his bible and begin to take in the words on the page, and before long he was absorbed. It was like reading a good novel you couldn't put down. This is when he would have questions for Patrick. Taking out his notebook he would write down the questions for the next day. While they worked in the garden, they would talk about God and the Word and before long the day had come to an end.

*****

Jonathon arrived at the Bordeaux House early the next day. He went to the shed in back of the house and began dragging out the tools he and Patrick worked with. He loaded the wagon and headed for the section they had worked on yesterday. Setting the tools aside he began to pack the plastic bag with leaves and sticks until it was full. He hoisted the bag over his shoulder and went to the front to set it on the curb for the trash collectors. Back at the flower bed, he began to clean around the plants as Patrick showed him. Not realizing how long he had been working he looked at his watch. *Where is everybody? It's almost 10 o'clock, and no one is here. It isn't Saturday. I wonder if something has happened or did they forget to tell me we weren't working today.* He thought with his forearm leaning on the handle of the shovel. He pulled out his phone and dialed Patrick's number.

"Hello," Patrick said.

"Patrick, did I miss something? I'm the only one here at the house. I've been here since eight this morning, but there isn't a soul around."

"Sorry, Jonathon, I guess you had better come over to our house. Something has happened."

Jonathon arrived at Rose Marie and Patrick's just as Patrick was calling Lance to see if he had heard from his mother. Hearing one side of the conversation, Jonathon looked at Rose Marie. "What's happened? Is A.J. alright?"

"Well, we pray she is. But no one has heard from her since Sidney saw her get in the pick-up truck with Nick," Rose Marie told him.

"Nick?"

"Yes. Nick is also being investigated," she said wishing she had not mentioned it.

"Investigated for what?" Jonathon said sitting down at the kitchen table.

Rose Marie handed him a cup of coffee then told him Sidney was investigating a ring of jewelry thieves and suspected Nick was involved. Then she asked as tactfully as possible. "Did you know the ring that Jeffrey gave Annabelle came from the French Market?"

"No. I didn't know he gave her a ring."

"I'm sure it was mother's ring," she said waiting for his reaction.

"What do you mean, mother's ring?"

"Somehow that ring, the ring I put in safekeeping for mother, ended up in a booth at the French Market," she said. "Jeffrey bought it for Annabelle for their engagement."

"I don't understand. How did it end up there if you had it in safe keeping?"

"Exactly, it was in the hidden compartment of the console table in the hall at the folk's house. Did you know about that hidden compartment?"

"No. What are you saying? Do you think I took it?"

"Jonathon, I don't know what to think. I know it's mother's ring and I also know where it was, so how did it end up in the market?" Rose Marie said with frustration.

"I didn't take it, Rose Marie, I didn't know anything about it or the table. As God is my witness, I did not take it. You do believe me, don't you?" he said with tears in his eyes.

"I'm sorry Jonathon. I had to hear it from you. If you didn't take it then it must have been Nick," she said relieved.

Jonathon felt betrayed, the one person he had always counted on was his sister, Rose Marie. It hurt deep within him as he realized his transgressions were once again coming back to haunt him. For Rose Marie to think that of him was understandable given what has transpired, but he was still upset by the accusation. Would he ever be trusted again by his family? Could he really put the past behind him? His involvement in an embezzling scheme of the Family Trust Fund was resolved in the courts. However, his family had not completely exonerated him. Not that he blamed them, but it made it hard for him to move on.

When Patrick finished his conversation with Lance, he came to the kitchen and poured a cup of coffee, asking Jonathon if he wanted a refill.

"Thank you, Patrick, I think I'd better go. I've got a head start on the flower beds, and I want to get back at it," Jonathon said putting his cup in the sink.

Kissing his sister on the cheek and shaking Patrick's hand he said goodbye and let himself out the kitchen door.

Patrick looked at Rose Marie with concern. She answered his look with an explanation, telling him what she had done.

"Don't you think that may have been a little harsh?" Patrick said.

"I told him I was sorry. I had to know, Patrick, and now we know it must have been Nick," she said justifying her actions.

"Just saying. He has been depressed lately, and your accusation didn't help any. I think I'll go help him in the gardens today. He usually has questions about scripture he's reading," Patrick said getting up from the table and putting his coffee cup in the sink next to Jonathon's. "I'll see you later," he said heading out the door, shutting it behind him without his usual goodbye kiss.

She went after him opening the door and calling him. "You didn't tell me what Lance said when you called him," she queried.

"He hasn't heard from her," Patrick said continuing to his car, and without further conversation, he got in and drove off leaving her standing on the landing at the top of the stairs leading to the patio.

Pulling out of the driveway and into the street, he took a deep cleansing breath to help with his feeling of disappointment in his wife's lack of judgment. Aware of the change in Rose Marie over the past several months, he tried to wrap his head around her lack of diplomacy. This wasn't the first time she had done something completely out of character. She dealt with A.J.'s lack of judgment on a regular basis, however dealing with Jonathon's had taken its toll on her. She and Jonathon were mere months apart in age, and as the two oldest, they were inseparable while growing up. He remembered the hurt she had when Jonathon was arrested, and Patrick wondered at the time if Rose Marie would ever be able to forgive her brother if he were proven guilty. Not knowing if her brother Robert was a believer before he died of a heart attack while Jonathon was in jail was another event taking its toll on her. Now another family crisis involving a sibling. Worried about Jonathon's mental state, Patrick turned onto the driveway of the Bordeaux house where he found Jonathon hard at work in the garden.

"Hello. I didn't think you were coming today. Everything alright with A.J.'s kids?"

"They haven't heard from A.J.," Patrick said putting on a pair of gloves.

"They seem to be level-headed and somewhat independent," Jonathon told Patrick.

"Yes. They've had to be. A.J. is totally irresponsible, as you well know," Patrick remarked putting his foot on the spade and lifting dirt from around a bush.

"Patrick?"

"Yes."

"Do you think my brother and sisters will ever be able to forgive me," he said looking at the flowers as he put them in the ground.

"Sometimes, I think we forgive someone for their sin, so to speak, but we don't forget the sin. You know what I mean?"

"I think so. I read in scripture that we should ask for forgiveness from those we've sinned against. I thought I had done that, but maybe I should do it individually. You know instead of just saying I'm sorry, I should ask for their forgiveness."

Patrick didn't comment as he let Jonathon study the subject on his own. Then, with concern for Jonathon's well being, he shared some scriptures that might help. "Acts 3:16 'Repent, then, and turn to God, so that your sins may be wiped out, that times of refreshing may come from the Lord,' and in 2 Corinthians 5:17 'Therefore, if anyone is in Christ, the new creation has come: The old has gone, the new is here!'"

"I want you to study these verses Jonathon and know that when you repent, your God and Father will forgive you," Patrick said.

On the way home later that afternoon Patrick thought about Rose Marie and wondered if her attitude may have something to do with her inability to forgive Jonathon. If that were the case, he would talk with her about it. Perhaps he could help her because he knew that once she forgave Jonathon a feeling of peace would come to her. He vowed to have that conversation with her.

Chapter **17**

Sidney left for his office after making Leslie promise to stay away from the studio and to keep Ryan occupied and away from his bedroom window on the chance that someone might notice him looking out at the studio.

Leslie went to her computer. Before putting her fingers and mind to researching more on Nick Nixon, she bowed her head in prayer. *Heavenly Father, I give you the glory and honor as I begin to look for information. I ask for guidance and discernment in my search. I pray that Your will, be part of my efforts and Father I ask for A.J.'s safety. Be with her children during this time. Guide us in our efforts to find her dear Lord. In Jesus' Name. Amen.*

Now that she had more information and especially since Sidney suspected that Nick was part of a ring of jewelry thieves she had more avenues to explore, court records, arrest records, and such. She was anxious to discover the connection with Beaux Bridge. Someone there had warned Nick, and she wanted to know who it was and why they were intent on letting Nick know someone was asking about him. Making a list of the people they talked to individually would be an excellent place to start. She began her search with the woman who gave them the information about Nick being a gambler.

When others on the swamp and in town were asked about this woman, they referred to her as "Mama." Leslie searched through the people they met including the Cajun on the bench that had talked to Sidney. She ran his name through only to come to a dead end. Everyone she looked up headed in the same direction. Back to the swamp. Not wanting to alert anyone in Beaux Bridge she hesitated to contact the police chief who supposedly was checking the archive records to see if there was any mention of Nicolas Nixon. *I guess it couldn't hurt to call and ask if he was making progress.* She thought as she dialed the number.

"Beaux Bridge Police Department."

"Hello, my name is Leslie LaRue Rye. My husband talked to your chief about a man named Nicolas Nixon. I'm calling to see if you have been successful in locating any information about him?"

"One moment please?" the clerk said

"Hello, Mrs. Rye, this is the police chief, I'm the one your husband talked to. Does he know you are calling me?"

"My husband and I work together in our P.I. business. Why do you ask?" Frustrated by his question, Leslie wanted to say, *I don't need my husband's permission,* but thought better of it and thanked the Holy Spirit for the reminder to keep a civil tongue.

"Someone representing Rye Detective Services called earlier asking the same question, and it wasn't your husband."

"Did he give his name?"

"No."

"That is very interesting. I'll talk to Sidney about this. In the meantime have you found anything that would help us locate this man and did you answer any of the person's questions when he called?"

"Being a good detective myself, I didn't give him any answers," the chief said.

"Do you know if it was a local call or could you tell?"

"I think it was a cell phone without a tracer. Because the number that showed up wasn't a working number."

"We've reason to believe that someone in Beaux Bridge contacted Nick and told him we were asking questions about him."

The chief picked up a pen and started making notes on his pad of paper. As the conversation continued, he asked Leslie some questions about the information they obtained while in Beaux Bridge. Although it was obvious the answers were guarded, he proceeded to ask.

"Who did you talk to when asking questions here in town?"

"I don't have any names. However, the one I'm most interested in finding is a woman people there call Mama. Would you know who that is?"

"I know of her, she is a fixture in our little town. She lives out on the bayou in a cabin. People say she knows everything that happens in the swamp. However, she doesn't take to the law very well, if you know what I mean?"

"Any suggestions on how to find out more about her?" Leslie asked hopefully.

"Not really, I know approximately where her cabin is but unless she comes to town, I probably wouldn't even see her. She is quite elusive, sly like a fox. She comes in like a ghost or spirit, usually after dark, here one moment and gone the next."

Leslie thanked him and asked that he keep them informed of any new developments and to please call if he found any other information in the archives of their records that would help them in their search.

She immediately called Sidney and relayed her conversation. Sidney found it interesting enough to want to send Charles to Beaux Bridge to do more snooping around since they wouldn't know him.

"I don't know Sid, I'm afraid that will push those in the know further back away from the information we could obtain. The chief seems willing to be involved in this. I didn't tell him about A.J., but maybe we should, so he can keep an eye out, in case Nick goes back to Beaux Bridge. What do you think?"

"Yeah, you are probably right about not sending Charles there, and if the chief is willing to work with us on this, he could cover his tracks better than we can."

"I sure would like to know more about this Mama character, she seems to hold the key since she knows what goes on in the bayou. Sid, are you going to tell the chief about A.J.?" Leslie said looking at her computer as if it could pop out the answer to her question.

"It wouldn't hurt. We can't put out an APB on her since she apparently went with Nick willingly and I have to have more proof of his involvement with a ring of jewelry thieves to have him arrested. This way we can kill two birds with one stone. In order to find A.J. we need to find Nick. I think the chief will take an interest in this if I tell him of my suspensions."

"Good luck, Sid. I'll keep digging. What about the men working on the studio? Maybe I should ask them about Nick." Leslie said

"Les, do not go there. You have their names. Research that but please do not approach them without me. Okay?" Sidney said knowing his wife was anxious to know what the men knew about Nick.

"You're right. I'll see what I can find out about them from my research. I love you." Leslie said knowing Sidney was right, *however, if it weren't for Ryan's safety…* she thought about her little boy and knew she would wait for Sidney to talk to the men working on the studio, again thanking God for keeping Ryan safe.

Chapter **18**

Annabelle and Jeffrey contemplated the events over the last few days. They even wondered if their wedding plans should continue in light of A.J.'s disappearance disrupting the whole family and now Rose Marie's questions about the wedding ring made planning a happy occasion upsetting.

"We're not going to let family matters interfere with our plans, Annabelle. You and I know that matters, such as these, work themselves out eventually. So, we will go ahead as planned. Since Rose Marie chose to attack Jonathon with her accusations of stealing mom's ring, I think it's time to ask him to be my best man. I intended to do just that all along. I just hope he doesn't think I'm asking him out of pity," Jeffrey said.

"Oh, I don't think he well Jeffrey. I think he will be very pleased. When are you going to ask him?"

"As soon as possible, but I want the time to be right, you know, not wrapped around anything else that might make him question my motives."

"Let's invite him to have dinner with us," Annabelle said enthusiastically.

"Great idea."

"Do you want to go out or have a special dinner at your place or even my place?"

"Interesting that we've two places. What are we going to do when we get married? I know," he chuckled. "When we get back from the honeymoon we haven't planned yet we'll say, 'your place or mine?' Decisions, decisions. We had better get started with these decisions, or we will find our backs against a wall."

"I've been thinking lately that the cottage in back of my home would make a great office for you," she said hopefully.

"One thing at a time. We're already on overload planning our wedding. Let's have dinner at your place, and I'll ask Jonathon to be my best man. In the meantime, we can go over brochures for our honeymoon. How does that sound?"

Taking Annabelle's hand, Jeffrey asked to pray for patience and clarity in the coming days as they made plans for their future.

Jonathon was curious after Jeffrey asked him to dinner at Annabelle's. Unnerved by Rose Marie's accusation, and still trying to move forward from his past transgressions, he was a little anxious about the dinner. He hadn't spoken to Rose Marie in several days, but Patrick was keeping him up to date on the A.J. and Nick situation as they worked in the gardens at the Bordeaux home.

*****

Not being sure where Annabelle lived and not wanting to look for a new address while maneuvering the streets of the French Quarter, he decided to take a taxi. He rang the buzzer at the gate and waited. Jeffrey came down the walkway toward the entrance as he said hello. After the gate was closed behind them, Jeffrey led Jonathon to Annabelle's home. As they passed through the screened-in area, Jonathon looked out at the cottage across the courtyard.

"That's a neat place, tucked back in here. You would never know it was here."

"Leslie lived there to write a book when she first came to the French Quarter. She and Sidney lived there for a while after they were married."

They went up the stairs where Annabelle greeted them in the open doorway. Giving Jonathon a quick hug, she invited him in. He was quite impressed with the surroundings as he followed Annabelle into the living room area.

"This is nice. Big, but homey at the same time. Who's harp?"

"That's Annabelle's, and she's good," Jeffrey replied.

"If I recall right, you play the piano very well also," Jonathon said nodding towards Jeffrey while sitting down in an overstuffed chair.

"We do make beautiful music together, after dinner we'll play for you," Annabelle said handing Jonathon a glass of wine.

"So, I guess you are wondering why we invited you here tonight?"

"I must admit, I'm curious."

Jeffrey looked at Annabelle, then turning to Jonathon said, "I'd like you to be my best man at our wedding."

Jonathon's eyes filled with tears as he stood and hugged his younger brother, then Annabelle. They all sat back down and

Jonathon, taking in a deep breath said he would be honored. He told them how grateful he was for their friendship and then quite unexpectedly, he asked for their forgiveness for any hurt he had caused by his past actions.

"Jonathon, let's leave that in the past. We forgave you a long time ago. Let's move on to a bright and wonderful future. We love you and thank you for excepting the role of best man." Jeffrey said with Annabelle nodding in agreement.

After the meal, as promised, Jeffrey and Annabelle played for Jonathon to his delight. He thanked them for a wonderful evening, but before calling for a taxi, he asked if anyone had heard anything about A.J.

"No. Leslie and Sidney are working hard on it. Since she went willingly, or so it appears, the law can't get involved. So our 'excellent detective team' is making it their project."

"How can they afford to do that? Who will pay them for all that work?"

"Don't worry about that. Sidney was already working on the ring of jewelry thiefs when he connected Nick to it. So he is still being paid, and Leslie has always done his research. In fact, Jeffrey hired her to check out Nick before A.J. ran off with him. So they are being compensated for their efforts."

"I'm glad. That did concern me. I'm happy you told me, Annabelle. Sidney was a real help to me while I was in prison. I owe him, and you, my life and my walk with the Lord. Sidney spent many hours with me, and I'll never forget it.

With that, Jonathon called a taxi and said his goodbyes to Annabelle while Jeffrey walked him to the gate. The brothers shook hands and gave each other a hug before Jonathon got in the taxi.

Chapter **19**

Not wanting to be seen on the main streets of Beaux Bridge, Nick turned his shiny red pick-up off the highway on to a less traveled dirt road that would take him to the bayou. He hadn't been down this road in many years, for that matter, he had avoided going anywhere near Beaux Bridge for close to thirty years. He knew he was taking a chance coming back now, but he needed to see Mama and find out what she knew and why she had given him up to the PI and his wife.

The road became rough with grooves from recent rains. He and A.J. bounced around like two rubber balls in a cage. When they came to a flooded creek, Nick kept going forging the water with A.J. screaming that she didn't know how to swim. Nick put the truck in gear and climbed the bank on the other side. Reaching the road of mud, the wheels began to spin. Nick held on to the steering wheel until the truck straightened and then hit dryer ground.

"Where are we going?" A.J. said with fear in her voice while holding on to the grab bar for dear life.

"Don't worry. We'll be there soon," he said watching the road for deep holes made by recent rains.

"I don't like this Nick. I'm scared," she said looking over at him.

"No need to be scared, little girl. I'll take good care of you. I'm not going to let anything happen to you. I just have to check out some things first, and then we will be on our way," Nick told her a little aggravated that she didn't trust him to keep her safe.

Not completely convinced, A.J. wondered if she had made a terrible mistake going with Nick. She was in too deep now to turn back. She thought about her kids and wondered if they were looking for her. Nick let her call them, then told her to get rid of the phone so no one could follow them. At the time she just did what he said, but now she began to think that was another mistake she made. Nick hadn't given her reason to not trust him yet, but things were not looking good as they drove deeper into the woods.

At times the road was so narrow, tree branches brushed against the truck making Nick angry. A.J. would duck as if to avoid the branches or more likely any fist she thought might come her way as Nick swore at the trees. Suddenly they came to a cabin nestled in a grove of cypress trees. Darkness fell on them even with the sun shining brightly. Beams shone through what little sky could be seen through the branches. Gauze like moss hung down from the trees out over murky water covered with green slime. He turned off the ignition and waited. An old women came out carrying a rifle pointed straight at them. A.J. ducked down, and Nick leaned out the window.

"Mama, it's me, Nick."

"Woo dat wit' u?" she said in a heavy Cajun accent.

"She's harmless. We're getting out of the truck now. Put the gun down," he said pulling on A.J.'s arm.

A.J. stayed behind Nick as they walked toward the old woman. She slowly put the gun down and waited for them to get closer. Nick pulled A.J. around so Mama could see her.

"Why on earth can't you leave the women alone? Why did you bring her? Now she knows how to get here. I don't like it," the old woman said in her heavy Cajun dialect.

A.J. couldn't understand a word the woman said. It was like she was speaking in a foreign language. Then Nick began to laugh and told the old woman,

"This girl is like a bowl of jambalaya, hot to the lips, spicy and full of surprises but warm to the touch. She could care less about this place. All she wants is me, so stop worrying old woman. We've some business to discuss."

They followed the woman into the cabin. A.J. looked around wide-eyed at what she saw. Alligator skins hung on the wall along with skulls. A lazy dog lay on the floor lifting his head only long enough to see who had come in. Mama leaned the rifle against the door- facing then went to the kitchen stove and taking a spoon stirred a pot of what smelled like a stew.

A.J. sat down at the table across from Nick. "Sure smells good, Mama. Alligator or catfish?" he said winking at A.J.

"Chicken. Dat de way to make de gumbo," Mama said giving Nick the eye.

Mama pulled out three bowls and ladled a serving from the pot into each bowl, then she spooned in some rice on the sides. Setting a bowl in front of A.J. she handed her a spoon. A.J. looked at the bowl then at Nick.

"It's really good. You'll like it, trust me," Nick reassured her.

Slowly lifting the spoon to her mouth just as Mama yelled "Det 'ot girl." But it was too late. A.J. burned her lips and put the spoon back in the bowl.

"She warned you," Nick said blowing on his spoon of gumbo.

"A little late, don't you think?" she said irritated. "Is she really your mama?"

"She's everybody's mama. Everybody in these parts call her Mama cause she takes care of them. Is'nt that right, Mama?" Nick said giving her an evil eye with an angry look on his face.

"Dat so, Nick boy," then looking at A.J. she asked where her children were. A.J. was surprised she knew about her children then Mama said. "De chirren day 'u leb."

A.J. felt Mama's judging eyes and felt a sense of shame. "Yes," she said under her breath.

Nick paid no attention to the connection between Mama and A.J. He had questions of his own.

"So why did you sell me out?" Nick said finishing the bowl of gumbo and getting up to fill another bowl. "Needs more file' you know," he said picking up the spice and pouring some on his gumbo.

Mama didn't say anything then motioned for A.J. to go outside. She took her bowl with her and went out to the porch surrounding the cabin. She sat down and began to finish her gumbo. Just as she put the last spoonful in her mouth, a big splash scared her, and she spilled the spoonful of gumbo down the front of her clothes. Looking outside the porch she was eye to eye with a very large alligator, and she screamed.

Nick came running outside and threw a rock from the ground at the alligator. He turned to find A.J. crying as she tried to clean herself up to no avail. He began to laugh at how pathetic she looked wiping gumbo off her skimpy top. Big tears rolled down her face smearing her heavy makeup. Her upper lip was swollen from where she burned it earlier. She was a sight to behold. Nick led her into the cabin to the sink so she could clean up. He went out to the truck and brought in her suitcase so she could change clothes.

What have I done? Why am I out here in this horrible place without a phone or money just waiting to be eaten by an alligator. I hate this. No man is worth this. She said as she tried to change clothes in what was a small closet-like space for a toilet. Thankful that it was inside she came back out to the room.

"Come on. We're leaving before it gets dark. Tell Mama goodbye."

She looked at the old lady. Mama gave her a look that pierced her soul. "Goodbye" she mumbled. She could have sworn Mama said to go back to her kids.

Completely foreign thoughts possessed her as they drove the same road back to the highway. She had always only thought of herself and what she wanted. Thinking of others did not come naturally. The fact that her actions might hurt others never entered the equation. Number one in her mind was A.J., hang the others. They were not important. Yes. She loved her children, but only on the surface. Her present thoughts were disturbing. What would happen to her kids if something happened to her? She admitted, she was scared. Scared out of her mind in the fact that her decision to run away with Nick could end very badly. Her thoughts also went to Jonathon. Her brother had followed the same path and look what it got him. How wrong she had been to blame him for everything that happened to her. Nick broke her silence surrounding her thoughts bringing her back to the present.

"You're awfully quiet," he said looking over at her sitting as close to the passenger door as she could get. "Do you plan to escape?"

"What do you mean?"

"You're in deep thought and have been since we left the cabin, and now you're sitting as far from me as you can. So, what are you thinking about?"

"I guess I miss my kids," A.J. said honestly.

"I really don't take you for being the motherly type," Nick said somewhat sorry for her.

"Why do you say that?"

"If you were more concerned about your kids, you wouldn't have come with me."

"Lance is nineteen. He can take care of the younger ones," she said ashamed of what she had just said. *Why would she put that responsibility on her son?* She thought.

"Do you regret coming with me? I thought you were excited about this adventure. Now you seem to have second thoughts. Was it because we went to see Mama?" Nick asked.

"Why would you take me to a place like that?"

"It never occurred to me that you would be frightened. You seemed worldly to me from the very beginning. You came on to me, remember. I just picked up on your clues," Nick told her.

A.J. thought for a moment about what Nick implied. *Was it that obvious?* Yes, she needed a man in her life to give her things and take care of her. She wanted the security a man could provide.

She never gave a thought to others in her life and what that would do to them. Her failed marriages were a direct result of her wanting more than they were willing to give. Was she spoiled like her brother Robert said? Was she incapable of taking care of her children and herself? Was she selfish not wanting to share herself with anyone?

Nick pulled into the parking lot of a small café. "Are you hungry?"

"Yes," she said looking down at the way she was dressed knowing men would look at her. Why was she concerned about that? She dressed this way to get their attention, and now she was worried about not looking presentable. It didn't make any sense.

They got out of the truck and A.J. followed Nick into the café. They sat down in a booth and picked up the menus.

"Nick, I think I better go home."

"Really? Why the change? We had a plan. Now isn't the time to change your mind, you're in it to stay."

"Are you saying I can't go back home?"

"I'm just asking what changed your mind?"

"I'm not sure. Maybe the way Mama looked at me. Maybe the way I looked at myself. I just don't know Nick. I feel different, you know what I mean?"

"No. I really don't. Mama didn't look at you any special way. I don't know what you are talking about. I just know that you've changed and I don't know why."

A.J. couldn't explain it either. Ever since they left the cabin, she felt different. Something had happened to her, almost as if she had been washed clean of her sins. *But how could that be?* She thought. When she left the cabin, she was at peace. She wasn't afraid anymore. It was probably just because she was glad to get away from the swamp and frightening views of the scene surrounding the cabin. Her thoughts went to her family and how they always took care of her even when she was rebellious. She could hear her sister Rose Marie talking to her about her kids. She knew she was right about most things, but she didn't want to hear it from anyone let alone her sibling.

A.J. had never experienced real fear. Maybe that was what happened, seeing how some people live but still have expectations of others, could have brought her face to face with her expectations of herself. Mama didn't approve of the way she was dressed or all the makeup on her face. But Mama lived in the woods with alligators surrounded by slimy green water. A.J. thought of the way she was raised in a very nice upper-class home with plenty of food and clothes and above all, love. She had thrown it to the wind as if it didn't matter that her family had given her the finer things in life. Now she was about to give that up for what? A red pick-up truck, a handsome man from the bayou?

They ordered their meal and ate in silence. After the waiter cleared the table and poured them another cup of coffee, A.J., holding her cup in her hands, looked at Nick and said. "Nick, this has nothing to do with you. It's about me. For the first time in my life, I'm ashamed of me, of who I've become. My kids deserve better. I've disappointed them and myself over and again. I want to start over and make things right."

"What does that have to do with Mama?"

"I think she let me know with a look, that I'm better than this."

"This, meaning what?"

"Running away from my responsibilities. Deserting my kids. It's time I grew up and thought about someone besides myself."

"I really can't take you back. I can put you on a bus. It's up to you. I don't have a hold on you. All I ask is you don't tell anyone about Mama or how to get to her place. Deal?"

"Deal. And thank you, Nick, for everything. I mean that."

"I know, your kids are lucky to have you."

"I hope they will be when I show them how much I love them," A.J. smiled ignoring the men staring at her.

"I probably should tell you this. Mama has a way of making people look inside themselves. While you were outside, she gave me a talking to. So, whatever Mama did for you, it's for your own good."

Nick took her to the bus station in Baton Rouge. Handing her a ticket, he gave her some money. "See you around," he said kissing her cheek. "Take care of yourself."

Chapter **20**

After Sidney gave a heads up on Nick. The police chief of Beaux Bridge was more cooperative. Leslie quizzed him about Mama and found out she wasn't only the "swamp mama" but was like a mama to many Cajuns living in the area. Curious about this woman, she began an intense search for her and her relationships starting with the swamp people she had met in Beaux Bridge.

She discovered that Mama had lived on the bayou all her life. Her daddy had made his living on the swamp. Her mother died when she was born, so her daddy raised her by himself. He taught her all there was to know about the bayou. She was nine years old when she killed her first alligator. She cleaned and cut the meat to sell to the cafés in the area. She learned how to cook by working in one of the cafes in town. By the time her daddy died, when she was in her early twenties, she was supporting herself and living in the same cabin her daddy built on the bayou.

Mama didn't have a real name or at least a name anyone knew. She attended weddings, helped birth babies and even raised a few when their parents died or deserted them. Never in trouble with the law but she was known to keep secrets and protect those who needed protecting. *If she was protecting Nick, why did she tell me and Sidney that he was a gambler owing people money and was accused of killing someone?* Leslie thought sitting back in her chair staring at the screen on her laptop. *Did Mama tell Nick that Sidney and I were asking about him? Is that why he left New Orleans in such a hurry? Did she know what he was up to?*

Leslie was getting a headache and went to make a pot of coffee. Looking out the kitchen window she saw the workmen in the back leave for the day. Annabelle and Jeffrey were coming for dinner to talk about the wedding and she had not a clue what she would serve. She opened the freezer compartment looking for something she could thaw. Standing with the freezer door open she felt someone behind her. Turning around she gasps. Standing there in her kitchen was one of the workmen.

"How did you get in here?" she asked sternly.

"The back door was open. I didn't mean to startle you. I knocked, but I saw you standing here in the kitchen. Is there a problem?" he said.

"I don't remember leaving the door open, let alone unlocked. What do you want?"

"I just wanted you to know we had the inspection today and we will be finished by this time next week," he said looking around the kitchen.

"My husband will be glad to hear that. He will be here soon if you want to talk to him," Leslie said.

"No. I need to go. The guy that used to bring us to work left town. My new ride is waiting on me, and I don't want to keep him waiting," he said leaving by the back door.

Leslie followed him and locked the door behind him making sure the slide lock was also on. Had she been so careless? She immediately went upstairs to check on Ryan. He and Daisy were sitting at the table putting puzzles together.

"Are you all right Miss Leslie?" Daisy said noticing her red face.

"Yes," Leslie said kissing Ryan on the top of his head. "A workman just came in the kitchen to tell me they will be through with the work on the studio next week. I was surprised that the door was open is all."

Not getting a response she went back downstairs and called Sidney.

"It may not be anything, Les. Just be careful. I'll be home shortly."

Leslie said, *thank you for your safekeeping, Father.* Then she remembered what the workman said about his ride. So it was Nick giving them a ride, and now he has left.

*****

That night after dinner, and letting Ryan tell everyone good night, the four of them began to discuss wedding plans.

"Jeffrey asked Jonathon to be his best man," Annabelle told them. "He was so pleased that Jeffrey thought enough of him to ask and very grateful to all of us for taking such good care of him during his jail time and through the trail. It was very sweet."

"Well, the attendants are in place. Who is going to perform the ceremony?" Leslie said writing Jonathon's name on her chart of things to do.

"We wondered if you would do the honors, Sidney?" Annabelle asked.

Sidney was a little taken back. "Are you sure? Wouldn't you like for Joe Sulley to marry you?"

"We thought about that. But after we saw how close Jonathon feels to you, well, we want you to marry us, Sidney. You and Leslie are our closest friends, and it just feels right. So what do you say? Will you marry us?"

"I'd be honored," Sidney said looking at Leslie.

"You can do it? I mean legally?" Jeffrey said.

"Yes. I can't say you are the first couple I've married," Sidney said smiling seeing the worried look on Jeffrey's face.

"Are you alright Leslie?" Annabelle said noticing how quiet her friend had been all evening.

"Yes. Why?"

"You seem preoccupied. Something bothering you?"

"Just thinking about the Nick mystery."

"Any word from A.J.?" Sidney said to Jeffrey

His cell phone began to ring, and Jeffrey excused himself going to the other room to answer.

"How do you know?" Jeffrey asked.

"Lance called and said she called him from the bus station to come and get her."

"Is she okay?"

"All I know is what I'm telling you now," Patrick said.

"Well, keep me posted. Let me know if you talk to her?"

"That was Patrick. He said that A.J. is back. She must have taken a bus because she called Lance to pick her up at the bus station." Jeffrey said coming back in the room.

"Well, that answers that question. Someone should talk to her about where she has been." Sidney said.

"Patrick and Rose Marie are going over to her place right now."

"Well, that is a relief. I hope she is okay. Shall we get back to wedding plans?" Leslie said.

Annabelle and Leslie were going dress shopping in a few days, and a cake tasting was set up for a time that both Annabelle and Jeffrey could attend. Satisfied with the plans, the couples said their good-byes.

Sidney closed the door behind their guest and went back to help Leslie clean up. He also noticed Leslie's mood and wanted to know what was going on with her.

"I wish I could talk to Mama again. I think she holds the secret to who Nick is. Don't you think it was weird how she sought us out and gave us all that information?"

"Yes. It was like she knew him. But why would she sell him out if she had nothing to gain? It was like she deliberately told us enough to get us interested in finding who he was or what he was doing? I don't know Les, we should wait to hear from A.J., she could be able to give us more information. I'm going to talk to Rose Marie and Patrick tomorrow and find out what she told them. Let's call it a night." Sidney said turning out the lights in the kitchen.

Chapter **21**

Glad that A.J. was back safe and sound, Katrina Louise hoped that everyone would return to the Bordeaux Homestead and finish preparing it to sell. Her investment was costing her every day it wasn't on the market. She made a list of things that still needed to be done and emailed it to everyone with a caption to get their attention.

TIMES A WASTIN'… PROFIT AT STAKE!

"Surely that will get their attention," she thought then pushed the send key.

Jonathon received the email and replied that he had been working all along on the garden and was sure he and Patrick could finish it in a few days. He suggested that he could begin painting the fence. He also suggested that they give A.J. time to rest after her ordeal with Nick. As much as he felt A.J.'s hatred toward him, he still loved her and had prayed for her constantly. He hoped that she was okay and would be able to come back soon.

Jeffrey was busy at work and planning their wedding but replied that he would be available on the weekends and some mornings and would let her know. He also told her that Jonathon never stopped working on the gardens and had accomplished a lot.

Rose Marie said she would be there the next day in the morning to finish the upstairs cleaning. Patrick said he would help Jonathon finish the gardens and then they could start painting the fence and checking for repairs.

The biggest surprise came from A.J. who said she would be there first thing in the morning to help finish the work in the garden and help paint the fence or start on the porch, sanding, cleaning and getting it ready to paint.

With everyone on board, the work began as everyone was enthusiastically committed to getting the house ready for sale. Everyone stayed clear of asking any questions about Nick. A.J. was grateful because she wasn't ready to talk about it. She would in time but right now she just wanted everyone to know she was willing and able to pull her weight and get the house in order so they could put it on the market.

Katrina Louise arrived and found everyone busy. She went to A.J. and gave her a big hug. "I'm so glad you are alright. I love you, sis," she said.

A.J. wasn't sure how to take Katrina Louise's concern. It felt nice to have her older sister express her feelings toward her. All she could think of to say was, "I love you, too." The words rolled off her tongue like butter. Where they came from, she didn't know, but Katrina Louise gave her an extra hug after the words were spoken. A.J. remembered how attentive Katrina Louise was during the Jonathon thing and how she never judged her. But this was different. Her sister was genuinely glad she was okay.

Later in the day as Jonathon, Patrick, and A.J. took a rest on the porch out of the heat. Jonathon handed her a bottle of cold water. She thanked him and then, without hesitation, she asked Jonathon to forgive her.

"What for?" Jonathon said surprised.

"For being so hard on you and yelling at you. I don't know why I act that way but going forward I'm going to try to be better and not so selfish."

"You are forgiven A.J., and I hope you will forgive me for any harm I've brought to you," Jonathon said reaching over and giving her a hug. "We both have some work to do on how we take care of our loved ones and perhaps we can work together on it," he said smiling.

"I'd like that. Someday I'll share some things with you that I've discovered recently," she said getting up and leaving the porch.

Patrick had been a witness to this conversation between them and asked Jonathon if he would like to pray. They both bowed their heads, and Jonathon began to pray. *"Oh Father, thank you. I've prayed for this miracle to happen between A.J. and me. You have blessed us with this reconciliation. Your almighty power has provided us with peace and security for us to build our relationship on and I'm so grateful. The hope of our salvation lies with you, Jesus. I ask your comfort for A.J. as she begins this journey. I pray she will find her way to you, her almighty Father. In Jesus' Name. Amen.*

Sidney was anxious to talk to A.J. to learn what she knew about Nick's whereabouts. Aware she was helping at the Bordeaux place, he drove over there hoping to find A.J. When he arrived he saw her leaving the porch. After greeting Patrick and Jonathon, he went to A.J. and said hello.

"Hi Sidney, are you helping us too. We've got a lot of work to do and could sure use all the help we can get. Katrina Louise has given us a great opportunity to get back some of what we lost in the family trust. I'm so grateful to her," she said scraping away at the paint on the pillars supporting the roof of the porch.

"You are doing a good job, A.J.," Sidney said noticing her appearance wasn't like anything he had seen her in before. She had on shorts that came almost to her knees and a sleeveless shirt that hung loosely from her shoulders. There was very little makeup on her face, and her hair was pulled back in a ponytail.

"Thank you."

"Actually I was wanting to ask you some questions about Nick if you are up to talking about it," Sidney said leaning against the railing.

"What do you want to know?"

"First of all, I'm glad you are alright."

"Thank you," she said, continuing to work.

"Did Nick agree with you leaving?"

"Yes. As a matter of fact, he took me to the bus station in Baton Rouge, bought my ticket and gave me extra money for my trip home," she said still scraping off paint.

"Did he treat you alright?"

"Except for taking me to the bayou, which was really scary," she said.

"Why did he take you to the bayou?"

"I really don't know for sure," A.J. said dipping the brush in the paint.

"Where on the bayou?"

"I really couldn't tell you, Sidney," she said truthfully since she wasn't sure how to get back to Mama or if she wanted to even try.

"Do you know where he was going when he left you at the bus station?"

"No. Someplace up north was all he told me when we left New Orleans."

"But you don't remember the name of the place?"

"He never said," A.J. answered.

"When you went to the bayou, did you meet anyone there?" A.J.'s hesitation gave Sidney a clue. So he asked her. "Did you see someone he called Mama?"

"I promised Nick I wouldn't talk about that," A.J. said not wanting to betray Nick or Mama.

"That's alright A.J. I'm just glad you are back safe and sound," he told her and not wanting to upset her said thank you and walked back down the steps to his car.

Sidney was convinced there was a strong connection between Nick and Mama and he intended to find out what it was. He knew Leslie was hot on the trail of Mama, and he planned to talk to the police chief again soon.

Chapter **22**

Nick, for some reason, felt good about letting A.J. go back home. After his talk with Mama, he realized it wasn't a good idea to have her tag along. Although he enjoyed her company, it was clear she was too close to the situation, and he needed to cut ties before she became entangled in something she knew nothing about. Now she had nothing to tell if asked. He still wondered about her sudden change after they left Mama. He was in his own thoughts after leaving the bayou and talking to Mama the day he and A.J. showed up on her doorstep.

Disturbing thoughts about that night long ago on the bayou haunted him once again. The night the law came looking for him telling Mama he was wanted for murder. Convinced all of that was in the past, all those years ago now, he was living his life, as usual, running with thieves, stealing things from the houses he worked in and selling the stolen goods in flea markets all over Louisianna.

Now wasn't the time to have a woman around his neck, so the opportunity came to let A.J. go without her wanting to know why.

He was going to have to lay low and hope the PI character didn't catch up with him. Knowing Louisianna like the back of his hand he knew exactly where to hide out as he headed for the Cane River. He knew it was risky, but hopefully, he wouldn't be recognized. Things had changed in this little town he thought as he crossed the river into town. Landmarks were gone replaced with new more modern buildings. He kept following the highway until he reached what he was looking for. When he pulled up to the side of the cabin a woman came out the door and with her hands on her ample hips and red hair pulled up in a bun she shouted:

"Old man Nick, what do you think you're doing coming here like you belong?"

"I missed you," he said laughing.

"Missed me? For all, you knowed I was dead and buried."

"Now Mercy, you know I love you. Always have and always will," he said walking closer giving her a smile that covered his face.

"Mercy knows better, you slime. What do you want anyway?"

"I need a place to stay for a few days, thought you could put me up is all," he said with a wink, leaning against the post holding up the roof over the front porch.

"The law after you again?"

"Maybe, don't know for sure, Mama just told me to lay low for a while."

"If Mama told you, then you better listen. She knowed things nobody knowed."

"Right, so can I stay?"

Mercy put her hands down and shaking her head told Nick he could stay as long as he stayed out of trouble and paid his way. Nick ran to his truck and got his belongings before she changed her mind.

"We've some catching up to do. You ate yet? Will come on put your things down and wash your hands so we can eat," Mercy said putting another plate on the table.

"What brings you to Natchitoches? I didn't think I'd ever see you again you knowed, after what happened here," Mercy said pouring him a cup of strong java.

"Boy, Mercy, this stuff will put hairs on a man's chest," Nick said ignoring her inquiry.

"You gonna' answer me or what?" she said sitting across the table from him.

"Can't rightly say. Just needed a place to stay and Mercy came to my mind. How've you been Mercy?" Nick said sipping the coffee.

"As if you cared. Nick, I knowed you. We grew up together, and now we're getting old. I cover my gray hairs with dye but look at you just letting them gray hairs shine. You don't never have a pride bone in your body. I'm still in the same place you left me. Ain't gone nowhere. Caught me a few men but none of them good enough to keep, so they got throwed back," she said tossing her head back and laughing.

Nick laughed with her trying not to feel her pain. Both of them were in their sixties now. Mercy was a real beauty when she was younger, but a hard life had done a number on her. Even though she tried to cover up the years it was evident that time had not been her friend. Several years back, when he returned to Natchitoches, they could have made it together, but Nick had a wild side that needed nurturing. He had never been able to settle down and had left many broken promises on the trail behind him. Looking at Mercy now he wondered if he had stayed would she have taken better care of herself or would she have resented him for being unhappy as he was sure he would have been.

Night-time came, and Mercy showed him where he could put his belonging in the spare room. Making it clear that it was where he would be sleeping. He didn't argue and told her thank you and said good night.

*****

The aroma of freshly brewed coffee woke him from the first real sleep he had experienced in days. Pulling his blue jeans on and slipping into his boots he headed for the kitchen.

"Sure do smell good Mercy," he said taking a piece of bacon from the plate.

"No shirt, no breakfast mister," Mercy said pulling biscuits out of the oven.

"Come on Mercy it's hot," he said leaning over to smell the biscuits.

"You heard me. Now go," she said swatting him with the kitchen towel from over her shoulder.

He jumped and went back to get a shirt. Coming back to the kitchen he barely got both arms in before sitting down at the table. He grabbed a biscuit and Mercy slapped his hand.

"Now what?"

"We're gonna say grace," she said bowing her head and holding on to his hand, the one with the biscuit in it. "*Amen*"

They sat across from each other not saying a word as Nick ate like he hadn't had a meal in a month of Sundays. Wiping his mouth and beard with a paper napkin, he looked at Mercy.

"That was a fine breakfast. You are an excellent cook, Mercy. Mama taught you well."

"Speaken of Mama she called last night after you done went to bed. Telled me why you was hiding out," Mercy said holding a cup in both hands, sipping the hot coffee.

"She did now? How did she know I was here?"

"I don't knowed. She knowed everything, Nick. You can't keep a secret from her you knowed that. She has a connection with a higher, what you say, power."

"What are you talking about, you crazy woman? Mama is the higher power. You know that."

"She follows someone higher than she is Nick and always has. Even when we was kids. Remember when she sent us into town to learn about God?"

"Oh, that."

"Yes, that. She told me she was going to set the record straight about the murder thing."

"What do you mean? What is she going to do?"

"I don't know, Nick. But you knowed once she gets her head set you can't stop her."

Nick helped Mercy clean up the kitchen while listening to her chatter on about people and things he wasn't at all interested in hearing. His mind was set on what Mama planned to do. He couldn't imagine her doing anything that would harm him, but lately, he wasn't sure she was in her right mind. Mercy had said something about Mama wanting to clear her debts.

Chapter **23**

Sunday morning found the Rye household getting ready for prayer meeting. Ryan was excited to see his friends and helped Leslie get juice and cookies prepared for their refreshments. Sidney was arranging chairs for the adults and getting song sheets ready. Soon people were showing up, and Leslie came out of the kitchen to greet them. Rose Marie and Patrick were the first to arrive, and Rose Marie asked if she could help with anything. She helped Leslie take the juice and cookies to the playroom for the children. Sadie and Joe Sulley were coming, and Sadie was going to teach the children.

When Rose Marie and Leslie went back to the living room, they were both surprised to see A.J. and her three children there.

"Is it alright that we came?" A.J. said looking at Rose Marie.

"Oh yes. We're so glad you're here, let me find a place for you all to sit," Leslie said leading them to chairs close to where Sidney would be teaching. She noticed they didn't have Bibles with them and went into Sidney's office to gather three Bibles. Returning, she smiled, then handed a Bible to A.J. and told the children they could share.

Rose Marie sat down beside Patrick. He put his hand on hers, and they bowed their heads as Sidney led them in prayer. *"Father in heaven, we praise your Holy Name and thank you for the blessing you give us daily. We also praise you for protection, keeping us out of harm's way. We're truly blessed on this beautiful Sunday morning to have new worshipers among us today. Our hearts are filled with joy as we worship together. I pray that the message I give today will be a tribute to your glory, Father. In Jesus' Name, we pray. Amen."*

"Our study today is on forgiveness. *Col 3:13 tells us 'Bear with each other and forgive whatever grievances you may have against one another.' Forgive, as the Lord forgave you,"* Sidney continued. "A peace surrounds us knowing that our Savior who died on the cross for our sins has forgiven us. That same peace comes when we forgive others and ourselves. We can remain victims of past hurts and resentments, or we can forgive those who have hurt us and move on, it's our God-given choice. When others do thoughtless, hurtful things to us, it's natural for us to become angry. But we soon realize that nothing positive comes from holding on to our past hurts."

Joe Sulley ended the meeting with a closing prayer blessing the food. Everyone said, "Amen," then standing, they left the living room and headed for the kitchen. Rose Marie went to A.J. and explained that the group had a potluck after the meeting.

"Oh, I didn't know that. We didn't bring anything," A.J. said.

"Don't worry about it. We have plenty and would love for your family to join us," Leslie said overhearing the conversation between the sisters then leading the way to the sideboard where people were putting the food out, buffet style. She handed each a plate encouraging them to join in.

"This is very nice," A.J. said to her children walking quietly behind her filling their plates.

Rose Marie and Patrick stood in line behind Lance who was instructing his siblings on the graces of serving themselves at the buffet since neither of them had ever experienced it before. Lance only knew because of banquets he had attended with friends. Rose Marie's heart swelled with praise and thankfulness watching her sister, niece, and nephews. *In God's time,* she thought, knowing the many times she prayed for them. She wasn't aware of what had happened to A.J. when she was with Nick, but she knew it was a miracle and she thanked God for it. The complete change in A.J. was almost overwhelming. Watching her now in a modest outfit and very little makeup she was overcome with gratitude.

"Good morning, Patrick," Jonathon said. "I never thought I would see the day. Did you?"

"No, I didn't. It just shows what faith will do, Jonathon," Patrick answered.

Jonathon found a seat beside Lance and struck up a conversation with him. They talked about Lance's job, the car he bought and paid for himself, and his plans for the future. Jonathon was pleased to be able to get acquainted with his nephew. He appeared to be a fine young man in spite of his upbringing, so far. It seemed things were taking a change for the better. Lance asked about the work they were doing on the Bordeaux house and asked if he could help. Pleased, Jonathon told him to check with his mother, and they could use all the help they could get.

After the meal, A.J. went to the kitchen to take her plate and found Sidney helping Leslie put out the desserts. "Sidney, I was wanting to know some other places in the Bible where it talks about sin and forgiveness," A.J. asked helping cut the pies and put pieces on the plates.

"Tell you what A.J., if you want to stay a while after everyone leaves, I would love to show you a study Bible and how to use it."

"Lance has to go to work if you wouldn't mind taking us home.," she said hopefully.

"We would be happy to take you home," Sidney said taking plates to the sideboard and announcing desserts were ready.

After everyone left, and the kitchen was cleaned, A.J. and Sidney headed for his study while her children helped Leslie and Ryan clean the playroom. Sidney handed A.J. a study Bible and began to show her how she could find a word or topic in the back and it would list scriptures for her to look up. Then he showed her the footnotes at the bottom of the page explaining the scripture and giving cross references from other scriptures. A.J. was very excited and interested in what Sidney was saying.

"Sidney, does God put people here who say…" she hesitated then continued "…give you a sign…or you know…that He's there?"

"Why? Have you heard from God?"

"I think so. But it wasn't Him exactly it was someone else… maybe it was an angel. She seemed to know me. Like she knew my soul. It was almost like she was telling me something, but she didn't say anything."

"Did this happen to you when you were with Nick?"

"Yes. Remember you asked me about Mama? It was her, she was the one that saw right through me with her eyes staring at me. Do you think God sent her?"

"Why do you think that, A.J.?"

"Because she made me look at myself, you know, who I really am and why I do the things I do. She made me sorry for the way I treat my kids. Seeing her, changed who I am or was, I don't know Sidney I'm really confused, I've never felt this way before. I feel shame, dirty somehow," A.J. said tears flowing down her face. "Do you think God will forgive me?"

"I know he will. When you truly repent and ask him to forgive you in the name of your Savior, Jesus Christ, he will forgive you. He's your friend, A.J., your heavenly Father. You can build a relationship with him that will bring you peace and understanding," Sidney told her seeing her pain. "You have a good start, A.J., coming to the prayer meeting this morning. I'll pray for you and help you know your heavenly Father. In Romans 3:23 it tells us that 'we all have sinned and fall short of the Glory of God.' But, A.J., freedom from past sins comes when we change and walk in the word of God and praise His Holy Name."

"But Sidney I don't know how to do that. I don't even own a Bible."

"You do now, A.J," Sidney said handing her the Bible where he showed her the way to find the things she had questions about.

"Thank you," A.J. said holding the Bible close to her chest.

When they left Sidney's office, A.J. showed the Bible to her children and told them they could all share until she could get them their own Bibles.

"Sidney showed me how to find things in this Bible that Jesus told us. So, we can look things up together," she said as they left the house to get in the car with the Rye family.

"We're so glad you came today and look forward to seeing you next week," Leslie said.

"We're glad we came too," A.J.'s daughter, Beth, said smiling.

After taking A.J. and her children home, Sidney and Leslie took Ryan to the park to play on the playground equipment. They sat next to each other on a bench watching Ryan.

"Did A.J. say anything about Mama?" Leslie asked.

"She was confused, but said she thought Mama could be an angel from God."

"Why?"

"This change that came over her was a direct result of her visit with Mama on the bayou. She said Mama saw right through her. Like Mama knew her soul, as she put it."

"Wow, that is powerful. What do you make of it?"

"Could be that God used Mama somehow to get through to her. Whatever happened on the bayou with Nick it changed who she thought she was and made her look at herself. Just the fact that she's seeking forgiveness is a miracle in my books. We really want to see that she gets answers to her questions. We never know what God's plan is or how he will work within us through the Holy Spirit, but you and I know, Les, that He's the one in charge," Sidney told her as Ryan came running to them.

"Are you ready to go home and eat supper?" Leslie asked Ryan

"Yes, I'm getting hungry," Sidney said to Ryan. "Let's go get a hamburger somewhere so mom doesn't have to come up with something for us to eat. Okay?"

"Yeah. But dad, you do the cooking sometimes," Ryan said in perfect innocence.

"Come on little man, before we get in trouble," Sidney said winking at Leslie.

Chapter *24*

"That is perfect Annabelle. It fits you to a tee and shows off that figure of yours," Leslie said a little envious. "Don't you agree?" she said to the sales clerk helping them select a suitable wedding dress in an uptown wedding dress boutique.

"It's not what I was thinking I would wear, but it's beautiful. Do you think Jeffrey would like it?" she said twisting and turning to see the dress clinging to her shapely body from every angle.

"I think he'll be surprised and pleased. It's not like anything you've ever worn, but Annabelle, it's so you. It's sophisticated, form-fitting, not too sexy, just right, and I love the champagne color. I'm telling you, you look gorgeous."

"I do like it even if it's a little out of my comfort zone. In front of clients and juries, I have to be so conservative that's why I wear suits most of the time. This is not conservative, Leslie," she said tugging at the material around her hips.

"So what's the problem?"

"I just want Jeffrey to like it," she said taking another look in the mirror.

"Let's put this matching vail with it and some jewelry," the sales clerk said.

After seeing herself with the vail and jewelry, tears filled her eyes and she said, "I love it."

*****

Their wedding day was fast approaching, and they still weren't sure about where to live. One night, while sitting in the courtyard, Jeffrey looked at the now empty cottage and reminded Annabelle of her suggestion that it would make a good office for him.

"You've never seen the inside of the cottage, have you?" Annabelle said, leaving the courtyard.

"Where are you going?" Jeffrey called after her.

"To get the key," she said running up the stairs.

Soon she was back and opening the door to the cottage. He followed her inside.

"Well, what do you think? Perfect right? We could put your desk right here in front of the window. You would have a place for your coffee pot and snacks or lunch without having to go to the big house. Come on upstairs. You could put shelves with books up here and a table for studying, and you would have the bathroom right there. Oh, Jeffrey, I think it would work. And, in the front house, I'm willing to get rid of some of my things so you can bring in your things to mesh with whatever is there already and make it our home. Can't you see how it would work?"

"Could we change the paint colors?" he said leading her on.

"We can do anything you want. I want you to be happy with whatever we do," she said holding her breath waiting for his answer.

"I think I'm sold. I can either sell my place or rent it out for income," he said thinking out loud. "But we don't have much time to get me moved in, so we better start making arrangements."

Annabelle put her arms around him and told him how happy she was that he agreed that this was a good plan. She would hire someone to paint the cottage and empty it out so that he could bring in his own furniture. She knew an auctioneer that sold high-end expensive furniture and art, one of her clients, and he would come and get anything they wanted to get rid of in both the cottage and the house in front and sell it at the next auction.

*****

Even though time was running out, with Leslie helping with wedding and reception arrangments, Annabelle was sure she could manage the rest of it. Since Jeffrey was still assisting his family at the Bordeaux house, it was up to her to get the ball rolling on the move. They picked a paint color, and Annabelle hired a painter. He would begin painting the next day and would be finished in time to move Jeffrey's office.

With the wedding one week away, stress was taking over for everyone. Leslie had a final decision on the cake and the flowers. Sidney was making sure everything was in order for the ceremony. Annabelle and Jeffrey had a massive case of the jitters but were ready to get married and go on their honeymoon to Paris. The Bordeaux family were on board and looking forward to the French Quarter's wedding of the year. Rose Marie was helping Leslie with the reception that would be held at Gallier Hall in the Pink room as Annabelle had dreamed about. But a small wedding ceremony would be held outdoors in a courtyard venue for just family and close friends.

*****

Last minute details were done, and now in a small room next to the wedding venue, Leslie was helping Annabelle put on her wedding dress. Zipping up the back of the gown they looked in the mirror. Leslie was always awestruck by Annabelle's natural beauty. Her dark hair, deep blue eyes, and beautiful cameo skin put her in a class of her own. However today that beauty gave way to the happiness that shown on her face.

"Oh, Annabelle, Jeffrey is going to be so happy when he sees you," she said straightening the vail that hung down over the short train giving a glimpse of the form-fitting champagne colored lace beneath.

"Thank you for all your help, Leslie. I couldn't have done this without you," Annabelle said leaning over to hug her friend. Holding hands, they bowed their heads, and Leslie said a prayer, "*Father, we ask your blessing on this day. We know everything is in your hands as Jeffrey and Annabelle exchange their wedding vows. Keep them safe on their honeymoon and bless their time together as they begin their lives as husband and wife. In Jesus' Name. Amen.*"

"Okay, are you ready? Let's do this," Leslie said opening the door to the outside courtyard filled with lush green plants flanking the aisle that led to the groom.

Jonathon walked Leslie down the aisle followed by Ryan carrying the pillow with the sapphire ring tied by a pink ribbon. He was the star of the show until the bride entered.

Every head turned to see Annabelle walking toward Jeffrey. The fabric of her dress flowed in the slight breeze with her vail laying over the train perfectly behind. Her beauty shone brightly under the hanging lights in the courtyard. Their eyes were fixed on each other as she slowly made her way down the aisle and stepped beside Jeffrey then handed her bouquet to Leslie.

Jeffrey stood mesmerized as he took her hand in his. Her outside beauty didn't mask her inside beauty that shone like a beacon. Her eyes expressed the deep love she had for him, and he inwardly felt an abundant sense of gratefulness to God for bringing them together.

Sidney began to speak to the couple telling them of the great blessing God gives two people as they become one in his eyes. He told of God's commandments regarding marriage and spoke of a love that is patient, reminding them to be kind, love each other as yourself. "For when we love each other as God loves us—with a genuine, sacrificial love—we will begin to know the meaning of true love, both received and given. Love each other in this way and remember that God blesses us with His unconditional love through our Savior Jesus Christ." Sidney concluded. Annabelle and Jeffrey read their own vows to each other and Sidney closed the ceremony pronouncing them husband and wife.

A.J. listened to Sidney as he talked of love not only in marriage but in all relationships with those surrounding us. She thought of her children and her siblings. She realized that it was hard to love others if you can't love yourself. *That's what's been wrong all along. I haven't been able to love myself,* A.J. thought choking back tears. *Going forward I vow I'll learn to love myself as I change who I've always been. I want to become someone others can love.* She said to herself as she stood with the others when Sidney introduced Jeffrey and Annabelle as Mr. and Mrs. Bordeaux.

Tears covered Annabelle's face as they embraced then turned to face friends and family. With Leslie, Jonathon, Sidney, and

Ryan following, closely they walked together back down the aisle. The rest of those in attendance fell in line behind them as they made their way to the street. Everyone waved white handkerchiefs in French Quarter tradition as they walked parade style to Gallier Hall a couple of blocks away with Annabelle holding an antique Battenburg lace parasol over her head. A small brass band wove in and out of the parade, then everyone surrounded the happy couple as they entered the hall.

*****

After the reception, they went out to a waiting horse-drawn carriage as well-wishers waved and shouted while the horse's hoofs clicked on the brick roadway as they rode away.

"It was a beautiful wedding and reception, wasn't it," Rose Marie said to her sisters and Leslie as they undecorated the Pink Room after the reception.

"Yes, it was wonderful, and now they are off on a honeymoon in Paris. How romantic is that?" Katrina Louise said with bare feet, after discarding her new shoes bought for the occasion. She and A.J. were putting centerpieces in a box.

"I really liked what Sidney said," A.J. shared not noticing her sisters looking at her.

"Yes. He did a wonderful job. A good message for all of us. Don't you think?" Rose Marie said.

"Yes. He did do a good job," Leslie said thinking about how blessed she was to be married to such a spiritual man. "Well, I think we're through and just in time, here come the guys to load the boxes into the car," Leslie said smiling as Sidney picked up a box.

"Did you send them off?" Katrina Louise asked knowing Jonathon had taken them to the airport.

"I did," Jonathon said with pride. "I've now officially completed my job as best man."

"Maybe not, Jonathon. These things need to go to their house, and I think you have the key," Leslie said with a smile.

"Oh yeah, I almost forgot."

Chapter **25**

The Wedding behind them, Leslie went back to work on her book, and Sidney continued to search for clues as to the whereabouts of the suspected leader of the ring of jewelry thieves.

With the construction finished on the studio she had moved her office and was enjoying the opportunity to write in peace and quiet. The novel she was working on was nearing completion, and her fingers were cramping from long hours of typing. With Jeffrey on his honeymoon, she didn't feel pressure to work on the Nick research. However, she knew it could help Sidney. Pulled between the novel she was working on and research concerning Nick Nixon she had decided to stick with writing the novel hoping for completion within the next few days.

The Beau Bridge Police Chief had called Sidney telling him that Mama had come to see him with a confession. She had told him a wild story about the girl on the bayou that supposedly disappeared. Her story took Nick off the hook for a murder that never happened. She told the chief Nick was guilty of many things, but murder wasn't one of them. Listening to the story, Sidney realized that it made more sense than the one told to them on their visit to Beau Bridge. He tried to call Leslie to tell her what he had learned, but couldn't get through, so he decided he'd wait until he got home.

On his way home, he went over the story again that Mama told the chief. Putting everything together he suddenly became aware of what the story meant. Now he was anxious to get home.

*****

Leslie was finishing the last chapter when her cell rang. Looking at it she didn't recognize the number, and since she was writing, she chose to ignore it. Ten minutes later the same number showed on the screen as the cell buzzed. Saving her work she pressed the answer key.

"Hello."

"Mrs. Rye?"

"Yes, this is Mrs. Rye. Who is this?" she said to the voice on the line that spoke with a Cajun accent.

"I name Mama, I talk at yo' an' you' manh bac' gone ago 'bout Nick."

"Yes, I remember. Do you have some information for me about Nick Nixon?" Leslie asked ready to write down any new information.

"I tol' you 'bout Nick. You de' time?" she said in her Cajun dialect.

"Yes. And I must tell you I have a hard time understanding you so could you please speak slowly?"

"I'd… talk… de'… slo'… miss…," then she began to tell the story of Nick Nixon.

She was present at Nick's birth. It was a difficult delivery, and his mother died. His father was never in the picture, and so she took him on to raise. He was an easy child, until his teens. He began to take things that didn't belong to him early in his life, but then it was outright stealing. She remembered one time turning him into the law when he was ten years old hoping that would cure him. He got in with a bad group of swamp boys and by the time he was seventeen he was out of her house and on his own.

He chased the girls and even brought a few of them home to live with the two of them. Then one night he brought a pretty young girl to the cabin and told Mama he needed her to stay for a while, then he left. She told Leslie that the girl stayed with her for over two months, and all she did was cry until one day Mama asked her why she was so unhappy. She told her that Nick had violated her and she thought she was pregnant. She thought he had left her with Mama because he was afraid she would tell the police. Mama found out where she came from and then in the dead of the night took her back to her town where she was safe. When Nick came back Mama lectured him on the facts of life and told him that "no meant no," and he better remember that. She told him not ever to darken her door again, and he didn't. The swamp people embellished the story of Nick leaving a girl with her and disappearing partly because they thought it was true and partly to get him in trouble with the law because he owed them money from his gambling debts.

"Did he know she was pregnant?"

"No," Mama said.Mama told her she never said anything to him until recently when he came back after she sent word to him that Leslie and Sidney were looking for him.

"But why now?" Leslie asked confused.

Taking a moment to be sure before answering the question Mama finally told her it was because she recognized her.

"What do you mean?" Leslie demanded, confused as to why this Cajun woman would know her.

Then, continuing in her Cajun dialect, talking really slow so Leslie could understand, Mama told her that she looked just like her mother did thirty-some-odd years ago.

Leslie gasp and then went silent. Her mind churned with every part of the story. She couldn't breathe as she began to put it all together one piece at a time.

"What are you saying?"

Mama told her what she didn't want to hear and how she didn't want Nick to be charged with a murder he didn't commit.

Leslie threw the phone across the room breaking it into a million pieces. Anger welt up in her as her face turned red and her heart beat increased until she could hear the thumping noise in her chest.

In great despair, she fell to her knees. *"Oh, Father, how can this be? Why have you put this burden on me? My mother was wise not to tell me the whole truth. What is your plan God? Why now? I could have lived my entire life without knowing this. What am I supposed to do with this information? This is an unbearable pain, not just for me, but thinking of my mother's pain. You are a sovereign Lord. You are the one I depend on. You are Almighty God, King of Kings, and Lord of Lords. Why have you brought this to me? I want to understand, I want to forgive, give me peace, Lord, now more than any other time in my life, and I need you. Oh, God. Why do I feel betrayed by you?"*

She lay prostrate on the floor crying uncontrollably. Sobs came from deep in her soul as the truth sank even deeper. Many things went through her mind like the flipping of fast-moving images from films projected on a screen. Always protected, seldom left alone, smothered with love, unanswered questions, time and again being told of God's presence, of God's will. Exhausted beyond control, she fell fast asleep on the floor in the studio.

Darkness covered the room except for the streetlight shining through a window casting a beam covering Leslie's body. Still sound asleep, she was unaware of the door to her office opening. A hand reached down and touched her waking her as she slowly recognized where she was. Looking up into Sidney's face, she took a cleansing breath. Somehow, he knew, and he lifted her limp body into his waiting arms. Neither one said a word as they held tight to each other. Her fear was slowly leaving, and she again felt safe.

"Where is Ryan?" she said concerned.

"He's with Daisy in the house," he said softly.

"My heart is breaking, Sid," she murmured.

"I know sweetheart, but with God's help, you will get through this. He promises to be with us, and he will be, Les."

Leslie was silent. *Was God with my mother? This was her pain, her secret, her shame. Was He there for her? What about Ryan? Would God be there for him? Should I tell Ryan the whole truth?* Thoughts swam around in her head. She had been so blessed and had never doubted that God was with her until now.

Chapter **26**

Several days had passed since her conversation with Mama. She went about her business letting the outside world think everything was okay. Inwardly she felt numb, void of feeling, it was like something had sucked the life out of her leaving her with an empty shell. She was functioning, but it wasn't really her, it was someone else, someone she didn't know. The smile that covered her face most of the time was gone, and she was sure it would never return. Even her thoughts were foreign and disconnected. One minute she knew what she was thinking and the next minute she wondered why that thought had taken over her mind.

Sidney was trying to be patient, letting her process her feelings and thoughts but he was becoming increasingly worried about her. With Annabelle still on her honeymoon, he couldn't rely on her friendship with Leslie to help her through this crisis. He would pray with her, and she wouldn't bow or close her eyes. She just stared into space. Exasperated, he called on Joe and Sadie thinking they could give her some peace. They tried, but nothing seemed to work.

One night at the dinner table, Ryan looked at Leslie and asked her why she was so sad. Leslie looked at him as though he wasn't there and didn't answer his question.

Sunday prayer meeting found Leslie in her room with a headache. When Rose Marie went to check on her, she found Leslie curled up in a fetal position in the dark with all the shades pulled. She sat on the edge of the bed next to Leslie.

"Leslie, is there anything I can do for you?"

'No."

"Let's pray together, Leslie. *Our Father in heaven thank you for being with Leslie. We ask for your healing, dear Lord. Give her peace and heal her body. Take away her pain and bring her comfort. We pray in Jesus' Name. Amen"*

Leslie didn't respond, and Rose Marie left the room. Leslie sat up and asked God if everyone knew her horrible truth? She wanted to scream. Her secret was her own and no one else. *Leslie, what are you saying?* She asked herself. Her thoughts went to Sidney and Ryan, and she began to cry for the first time in days. *Where is Annabelle when I need her?*

Sidney came in the room and saw Leslie sitting up in bed crying. He went to her and held her tight. "Does everyone know?" Leslie asked between sobs.

"No. they just know you're not feeling well, and everyone is concerned about you. So am I, Les. I've never seen you like this. Please let me help you. God hasn't forsaken you. Remember his promise, to be with you through the hard times. Talk to him, Leslie. He will be there. He never promised a life without challenges. With his help, you will get through this. Please, Les, God loves you." Sidney said pleading with her.

Leslie stopped crying and put her head back on the pillow. Still holding Sidney's hand, she promised to try. He leaned down and kissed her forehead.

"I need to go back downstairs. Are you sure you're alright?"

"Yes, thank you, Sid. I love you."

"I love you too sweetheart. I'll see you in a little while."

Leslie thought about what Sidney said. *Holy Spirit, what is God's plan? What was his intention when I was born? Why was I born? Why did my mother die? Oh, Father please tell me why. I just want to understand,* she prayed.

Suddenly she looked up, and there was Annabelle right there in front of her like a mirage, an answer to a cry for help.

Annabelle came to her bed and sitting beside her put her arms around her, rocking back and forth in silence. Leslie felt her friendship, her all-knowing, her faith in God. Her tears dried, her emotions settled as she began to share her despair in detail leaving nothing out. All the grief of the information she now held came out like a flood as Annabelle held her hands and nodded. She admitted her anger with God, her unanswered questions as she pleaded for peace. "Why, why," she finally said to Annabelle.

"Leslie, how many times have we questioned why? How many times have the answers come without us knowing? We don't have to know God's plan to know that he has a plan and keep remembering that no matter what, He's always with us. Jesus died for our sins, and the sins of others, Leslie. You're a child of God. You believe in our Savior, Jesus Christ, and that he died on the cross. You know the grace of God is with you. He understands the pain you're in more than you or I will ever understand. Don't you know He grieved the loss of His Son?" Leslie nodded in agreement. "God has brought you closer to Him, building a relationship so He could trust you with whatever is in store for you and everyone involved. I understand A.J. was led to learn more about forgiveness and sin through the same woman that shared her secret with you. Through this woman called Mama, He has brought the two of you face to face with your past. The fact that Nick is involved shows the depth of God's plan for salvation not just for A.J., but for Nick."

"But…," Leslie stammered.

"No buts, Leslie, you know what it takes to bring others to believe in our Savior. As a believer, you will show them the peace that comes with faith. God wants His child to stand firm just like you did with me. Forgiveness is a beautiful thing, Leslie. You made me see that, and now you have a chance to show someone else the power of forgiveness."

Leslie lowered her head and began to pray to her Heavenly Father. *"Father you are my anchor, my solace in my despair. Your glory rises far above this sinful world. Thank you for my salvation and your grace. Please forgive me, Father? I'll go where you lead me, Lord. Your will, through me, will be done. In Jesus' Name. Amen"*

Chapter **27**

Mercy and Nick sat on the porch out of the heat coming from the cook stove in the house. Silently they watched as fireflies showed their beacons and frogs from the lake made their presence known.

"What do you think Mama meant when she said she was going to take care of her debts?" Nick said staring at the sky above the trees filled with stars.

"I don't rightly knowed," Mercy said with her eyes closed.

"It's know not knowed. Why do you always put an 'e-d' on the end?"

"Hey, don't talk to me about that. It's not that you're so perfect Mr. Hiding-from-the-law," Mercy said not opening her eyes.

"I'm just sayin'."

"Hush. I don't want to hear it. For someone with a past like yours, you shouldn't correct no body else. I knowed… know things about you that you should be ask'n God almighty to forgive you."

"God Almighty? Since when have you gotten so religious?" Nick said looking at her.

"I'm not religious. I do believe in God. If that's what you mean. You make it sound ugly. What is wrong with you Nick? You and I was raised by a Godly woman. What happened to you?"

"Wait a minute. You're not lily white yourself."

"Yeah. But when I talked to God about it, I knowed I had to change and tell him I was sorry about the sinful things I did."

"Really, that's all it took?" Nick said laughing.

Mercy was silent. She got up and went back into the house and to her room where she shut the door. Leaning with her back to it she asked God to forgive Nick.

Nick stayed outside a long time trying not to think about what Mercy said. He was thinking about what Mama said, and hoping she wouldn't do anything foolish. He wanted to go inside and tell Mercy he was sorry he upset her, but she would probably just start talking to him about God again, and he didn't need that right now. He got along okay without God, and he wasn't going to mess things up by relying on Him now. Anyway, he was in too deep. God probably wouldn't take him in, being damaged goods and all. Even if he wanted God in his life, he wouldn't know where to start. *What's wrong with you, man? Why are you thinking about God? You should be figuring out what to do next. You can't stay here much longer. I wish I knew what Mama was up to.*

The next morning found Mercy sitting on the porch with a cup of coffee. She heard Nick in the kitchen but didn't get up to fix his breakfast like she had done ever since he arrived. In a little while, he came out on the porch with a cup of coffee and a piece of toast.

"We're not having breakfast, I see," Nick said biting into the piece of toast.

Mercy sat with one knee bent and her foot resting on the chair quietly drinking her coffee.

"Look I'm sorry I upset you last night," Nick said leaning against the railing looking down at her clean washed face, and straight wet hair draped over her shoulders from a shower.

"Are you really? Or do you just need a place to stay?" She said not looking up at him.

"Now Mercy, don't be that way. I said I was sorry," he said sitting down in the chair next to her.

"What are you sorry for, Nick?" Mercy calmly asked.

"Well, I guess for correcting you."

"And?"

"Oh yeah, for teasing you about being religious and the God thing."

The morning sun was shining through the leaves on the trees casting shadows on the porch. Different species of birds began their songs, but Mercy had nothing to say. They sat like two strangers rocking back and forth, watching squirrels scampering about, and the neighborhood cat lying in wait to chase an unsuspecting prey. Finally, Mercy broke the silence.

"She told me what you did."

"She did?" he asked anxiously.

"She said you was wrong, but you wasn't no murderer."

"Well, she needs to mind her own business," Nick said getting up and going back in the house slamming the door behind him.

Now he knew for sure what Mama was up to, and he had to stop her before she got both of them in a lot of trouble. He packed his belongings and came back out the door with his suitcases.

"Thanks for putting me up, Mercy. I'll see you around sometime," Nick said jumping off the side of the porch throwing his things in the back of the truck. He waved as he backed the truck out onto the street.

Mercy didn't wave or smile, she just prayed that he wouldn't do anything he would regret later. *"Keep him safe, Lord,"* she said watching him stop at the corner and turn toward town. She went back in the house for another cup of coffee, and as she reached for the coffee pot, she saw a hundred-dollar bill stuck under the coffee pot.

Chapter **28**

eslie was taking time away from her writing to study her Bible. After Ryan went to bed, she and Sidney spent time together reading scripture and talking about what it meant to them. Peace was coming back to her as she trusted in the Lord, her God. At times she worried about her anger and how it had pulled her away from God. She knew that Satan found a weakness and took full advantage of it. They talked about the discipline of studying God's word and how living for Him was the foundation of a good relationship.

Annabelle and Jeffrey were busy selling Jeffrey's house, and making Annabelle's house a home to both of them. The office in the cottage was working out better than they thought. Back from their honeymoon only a few weeks they had settled into married life. They were now ready to entertain.

"Hi Leslie, I was just getting ready to call you. Jeffrey and I would like you and your men to come over for dinner. We can make it early so Ryan can keep his bedtime."

"Oh, Annabelle, that is sweet. We can ask Daisy to stay with him, then you won't have to start dinner so early. That way we will have more time together."

Date and time set, Leslie told Annabelle how anxious they were to see what they had done to the house and especially the cottage.

"You won't recognize it, Leslie. It's very masculine, and Jeffrey loves it."

"I'm so happy for you two. We haven't heard about Paris yet either, so we'll have a lot of catching up to do."

When Sidney and Leslie arrived, Jeffrey went to let them in at the gate. As they walked towards the courtyard, they talked about how Annabelle was anxious for them to see everything they had done to the house and to the cottage in the back. Annabelle was waiting for them in the courtyard. She gave Leslie a hug and put her arm around her as she led her to the cottage. When they entered the cottage, Annabelle waited for their reaction.

"Wow. This is a complete turnaround. I love the color, and your desk fits perfectly, Jeffrey. The pictures, lamps, leather chairs. It just doesn't look like the same place." Leslie said turning to see everything.

"Wait until you see the upstairs," Annabelle said starting up the stairs.

"Oh. Look, Sidney, a library and what beautiful bookcases," Leslie said going over to look at the books.

"I like this mission-style library table and chairs," Sidney said to Jeffrey. "This is a great place to work and like Les said, it's not the same place."

Jeffrey and Sidney went back downstairs and out to the courtyard. Leslie and Annabelle stayed behind. Sitting at the library table, Annabelle asked Leslie how she was doing.

"Much better. Did I tell you I talked to my aunt?"

"No."

"I asked her what she knew about everything."

"Did she know what happened?"

"Sort of. She didn't know how much I knew. So at first, she didn't say much. Then I told her about the call from Mama. She filled in a few of the blanks. Like the fact that my mother was reported missing, and soon everyone assumed she was dead. She never told them who had raped her or where she had been. She just showed up one day. Then my aunt told me how sorry she was about everything. We talked about my mother and why she didn't want me to know the truth about my birth and my father."

"Did you get some clarification?"

"I think so. I now know why my aunt always protected me. She was always afraid that if my father found out about my mother's death that he may try to come and get me."

"But he didn't know about you or that your mother was pregnant."

"Exactly. But she didn't know that, and my mother never told her the whole story or who the father was."

"Oh, so did you tell her?"

"Yes. And she knows who he is because he did some work for her neighbor and was arrested when her neighbor was missing some expensive jewelry after he worked for her. So, he was right under her nose, and this was when my mother was still alive."

"Did she ever see him again?"

"No."

"So now Sidney has another lead."

"What happens if Sidney finds him? Do you want to confront him? Are you ready for that?" Annabelle said concerned.

Leslie sat quietly not answering Annabelle's questions. She had gone over in her mind, what she would do if she ever had the opportunity to come face to face with the man that she found appalling, the man that supposedly is her father. She knew the Bible tells her to forgive, but she wasn't ready for that yet and didn't know if she could forgive him. *What would my mother want me to do?* She thought.

Before she could answer Annabelle, the men in their lives called to them to come down.

"Did we plan to eat sometime soon?" Jeffrey said taking Annabelle's hand as she came down the stairs.

"Yes. Let's go to the house. Everything is ready we just have to put it on the table."

Sidney took Leslie's hand, and they followed them to the house where again they were surprised at the changes that had been made. Jeffrey's furniture blended well with Annabelle's and the arrangement changed the whole look of the room.

"I like it. It honors both of you. How do you feel Jeffrey?" Leslie said looking around the room.

"It's our home. I love coming back here after a day at work in the cottage. The whole thing is perfect. It's the best decision we've made," he said winking at Annabelle as she and Leslie brought things out to the table.

The meal almost over, Sidney's cell buzzed. Excusing himself, he got up from the table and went into the kitchen to answer a call from Daisy.

"Mr. Sidney, I'm sorry to call you, but Ryan is very upset. Something about seeing your bad guy. He doesn't want to go to bed until you come home. He's crying and shaking, and I don't know what to do. I've never seen him like this."

"Let me talk to him?"

"Hello," Ryan said in between sobs.

"Son, this is your dad. What's going on?"

"I saw him, dad. He went to mom's office and looked in the door. Then he went to a window and looked in there," he said with his voice trembling.

"Are you sure it was him, Ryan," Sidney said in a low voice, so Leslie wouldn't hear him.

"Yes, Dad, it was him. Please come home. I'm scared, Dad. What if he comes in the house? I don't know how to protect Daisy."

Sidney smiled at his son wanting to protect Daisy. "It's alright Ryan, I'll be right there."

Sidney hung up the phone and went back to the table where everyone was deep in conversation and hadn't heard him talking to Ryan. Making some excuse about a problem he needed to take care of he apologized and said he would be back later and take Leslie home. Everyone seemed to accept his explanation, and he headed out with Jeffrey following him to the gate to let him out.

"Is everything okay?" Jeffrey asked noting Sidney's hurry.

"Yeah. I'll be back in a little bit."

Leaving the French Quarter, he headed for the Garden District. Turning down St. Charles he watched for Nick's red pickup. As the trolley passed by, he thought that Nick could park somewhere else and ride the streetcar to and from. He pulled into the back alleyway behind the studio with headlights off and engine idling. He looked around to see if everything was clear. Putting it back in gear he pulled into his parking place and turned off the engine and got out of the car. Keeping an eye on the area around him, he made his way to the back door of the house. He put the key in the lock, then he noticed a reflection behind him through the window pane in the door. Slowly turning around, he saw a figure run down the alley. Without hesitation, he took off after the runner. Pushing to keep up, he realized he was a bit out of shape, as the runner kept running. Finally catching up with his subject, he tackled him, pinning him to the ground. He turned him over. It wasn't Nick.

"Who are you," Sidney said holding him to the ground. Soon it was established that the man he had chased and tackled was out for a run.

"Did you see anyone hanging around the studio in the back of my house?" he asked as he helped the man slowly get up.

"No. I'm the only one out here, well, except for you."

"I'm sorry man. Are you alright?" Sidney said concerned.

Making sure the runner wasn't hurt they shook hands, and both men walked away in opposite directions. Sidney still breathing hard wasn't as sure as the other guy about his injuries. Stretching his shoulders and neck, he went back to the house and opened the back door locking it behind him. Calling to Daisy, then to Ryan, he got no answer. He looked around but didn't see anyone, then went upstairs two steps at a time. When he got to Ryan's room, he found the door locked.

"Ryan are you in there? It's dad. Open up son," Sidney said anxiously then frustrated, he knocked on the door again.

Slowly the door opened, and Ryan ran to Sidney throwing his arms around his legs.

"It's alright Ryan," he said patting his son on the head. "Are you alright, Daisy?"

"Yes, I'm fine Mr. Rye."

"Let's go downstairs, and I'll take you home and Ryan you can go with me to get your mom at Annabelle's."

After taking Daisy home, Sidney began to question Ryan to understand exactly what he saw. Feeling safe with his dad, Ryan began to open up.

"I was looking out my window at the stars when a saw someone move out back. I turned out my lights and looked again. I saw him standing at the door looking in with his hands up like this," Ryan said showing Sidney. "Then he went to the side of the office and did it again, you know with his hands up to his eyes."

"Then what did he do?"

"He turned and walked down the alley."

"Did he run or just walk?" Sidney asked.

"I couldn't see him. He went behind the building."

"Are you sure it was the same man you saw before?"

"I think so dad, it was dark, and he never turned around, so I could see his face. He was wearing shorts."

"Shorts like someone who was exercising maybe out for a run?" Sidney said thinking about the guy he tackled in the alleyway.

"Yeah, like on TV when they run a race," Ryan said excitedly that his dad believed him.

It took some convincing, but Sidney finally convinced Ryan that the man he saw from his window was indeed the same man that Sidney tackled. He was probably just curious to see what the inside looked like but without lights, he couldn't see inside. He told Ryan. Then he told him how brave he was and thanked him for protecting Daisy.

Leslie was surprised to see Ryan when Sidney came back and let Ryan tell the story with everyone listening.

"Dad said I was brave, mom."

"That you were Ryan, good job. Now we had better get you home and to bed. Thank you for a fine dinner and the tour of everything you have done here," she said to Annabelle. "I like it very much. I must admit I'm a little jealous of your office, Jeffrey," Leslie said giving Ryan a little push toward the door.

After securing the gate, they walked down the sidewalk toward Jackson Square where Sidney had parked the car, with Leslie holding Ryan's hand. *Oh, Father thank you for keeping our little boy safe,* she prayed to herself. He's terrified of Nick, and he doesn't even know his true identity. These thoughts disturbed Leslie, and when she looked at Sidney, she could tell he was thinking the same thing.

Chapter **29**

The Bordeaux house was coming along, well on its way to being listed. Lance and A.J. worked side by side planting, painting and anything else that needed to be done. Lance and Jonathon were growing closer, and Patrick had become the leader of them all. He was pleased with the relationships that were being mended with each other and with their Lord.

The only sad note among the siblings was Rose Marie and Jonathon. Ever since the night that Rose Marie accused Jonathon of stealing the Sapphire Ring that belonged to their mother, there was a wide distance between them. Hoping that they would work things out themselves, Patrick had not mentioned it to Rose Marie. However, he felt the time was now to bring them together and solve the issue separating them.

Jonathon had been coming to a prayer meeting at the Ryes, but Patrick still saw the strain between his wife and her brother even at Sunday prayer meetings. Rose Marie had taken A.J. and her family on as a continuing project, and she was not spending time with Jonathon. On the outside, Jonathon seemed alright with the situation, but Patrick suspected that privately he was still very hurt and didn't know how to deal with Rose Marie.

"Patrick, I'm so happy A.J. has found Jesus. She and her family are so much happier," Rose Marie said on their way home from working on the house.

"Yes. She's making good strides, and it's showing on her kids. Lance is a real hard worker and enjoys being with the family," Patrick commented. "He and Jonathon are building a great relationship. It's good to see. They talk about God, Lance's job, and how he's doing at the university."

"Yes, I was surprised that Lance is going to the university at night. I don't know how he finds time to help us at the house and work too," she said.

"Jonathon has been helping him with his classes. It keeps Jonathon busy because he has to study too. I think it's good for both of them. I'm proud of Jonathon. He has come a long way," Patrick said hoping that talking about Jonathon would open the door to talk to Rose Marie about the distance between her and her brother.

"I'm glad Jonathon has something to fill his lonely hours," she finally said. "He has always been a loner even growing up, he was always off by himself."

"Have you forgiven Jonathon?"

"For the family trust, you mean?"

"Yes, what else would there be to forgive him for?" Patrick said. "Surely you don't still think he stole your mother's ring."

"No. I'm sure he didn't. I just don't know how to mend the fences between us. I know I was wrong to accuse him, but I don't think he has forgiven me for my accusation," she said.

"Do you think it might help to ask Jonathon to forgive you?" Patrick said waiting for her answer.

"I said I was sorry," she said.

"Maybe that's not enough. If you're serious about mending fences, then perhaps you need to go a step further and ask for his forgiveness. And, honey, it will go a long way toward your feelings about everything and give you some peace."

"You're probably right," she said knowing Patrick was being patient with her but wanted her to see she had a part in making the relationship with Jonathon better. So, she promised herself to have a talk with Jonathon soon.

*****

The day had finally come, and everyone was gathered in the Bordeaux house parlor to make sure the house was ready to go on the market. As usual, Katrina Louise was late. Jonathon and Lance were talking about the homework for Lance's class at the university and A.J. was asking Patrick about things she was reading in the Bible. Rose Marie watched her family interacting with each other and thanked God for answered prayer. For years she had prayed for her family to know Jesus as their Savior and now she realized it was in God's timing not hers. A tear ran down her face as her heart swelled at the thought of her siblings coming to know God and relying on Him in their need. She knew that Jonathon had found Him and now A.J. was on her way to her salvation.

Suddenly Katrina Louise waltzed into the room apologizing for her tardiness. They all laughed knowing this was not unusual behavior. With a flip of her hair, she ignored their implication.

"Okay. Let's go down the list of last-minute chores, and then we'll talk price," she said pulling her notepad from the briefcase.

After the list was reconciled and assignments to put final touches on the house were made, Katrina Louise laid out the papers showing comparisons of other properties that had sold in the last few months. Then she told them the price she would put on their house. She gave each one a paper with the figures including the amount she paid and the cost of materials. There was a collective gasp at the large figure at the bottom of the page.

"As you can see, we stand to make a good size profit, and that's because we, as a family, have worked together and made this happen. I've no doubt that we'll have offers above and beyond the asking price because we've made this a showplace. So, you can pat each other on the back for a job well done," she told them as they all began to clap.

"One more thing. I talked to Annabelle, and she has talked to the Judge in charge of Jonathon's case, and if we sell this house for the amount we're sure to get, his obligation to his sentence will be complete," she said looking at Jonathon while everyone cheered and went to hug him.

"I love you Jonathon, and I'm proud you. Will you forgive me for any hurt I put on you?" Rose Marie said.

Jonathon gave her a big hug and whispered in her ear. "You're forgiven Rose Marie, and I love you. I thank God you're my sister."

Chapter **30**

eslie was trying to come up with a fun birthday party for Ryan's fifth birthday. Talking about it with Daisy, she had thought about having it at a park. Daisy told Leslie that a birthday in their spacious side yard would be exciting for Ryan. He could have his friends there from his play school.

"What a great idea, Daisy," Leslie said.

Leslie got excited about renting a bouncy ball house. And she knew of a place that rented merry-go-rounds with cars instead of horses. She could have the bakery make a cake with a carnival theme and hire a clown. She wanted it to be a surprise, so she and Daisy kept the plans quiet.

That night after Ryan went to bed, she told Sidney of their idea.

"So, what do you think?" Leslie said.

"Sounds great. I know a guy who makes animals out of twisted balloons. Maybe some of the guys in the prayer group could help me make some booths for the refreshments like they have at carnivals. We could even have games. I think this is a great idea, Les. And Ryan will be blown away. I do see one issue with it."

"What? It's perfect," she said.

"How do we top it next year?" he said laughing at the puzzled look on Leslie's face.

"You have a point, but no matter, we'll go ahead as planned. Okay?"

"Maybe we could reel it in a little bit this year and add something to it each year until he outgrows it or wants something different," Sidney said.

"That's not a bad idea. Then he would look forward to the next year to see what was added. I like that Sid. Besides, it could be a little overwhelming at his age, and he may not even appreciate it. As he gets older, he would have more fun."

"So, let's have the same theme just down to a five-year-old size. So, for sure, the bouncy house, and one clown to hand out prizes, and a carnival cake. Do you think that will be enough?" Leslie asked.

"Maybe instead of a carnival cake you could make a King Cake, you know with the plastic baby inside and the colored icing on top," Sidney suggested.

"Oh, Sid, the kids would really like that," Leslie said writing it down on the notepad she had retrieved from Sid's office.

"Would it be too much on you to make the cake?" Sidney suggested.

"No. I can make a big one and with the other refreshments that will be plenty," Leslie said adding it to the list

With all the plans a go, she talked to Annabelle and asked her to go shopping with her at the party store. Most of the party stores were stocked for Mardi Gras, but one store in uptown New Orleans had more birthday party things that were age appropriate.

"Who came up with this idea?" Annabelle asked as they gathered prizes for the party.

"It was Daisy's original idea to have it in the side yard. Then Sid and I got our heads together, and here we are," Leslie said putting a bag of balloons in the basket. "I wonder who is going to be able to blow all these balloons up."

"It will have to be a team effort," Annabelle said laughing with Leslie. "It's good to see you laugh again. You haven't heard anything else about Nick have you?"

"No. It's like he disappeared off the face of the earth. Sidney told his client that he didn't feel right pursuing his search any longer on the client's nickel and told him he would give the information to the DA and let them take it from there. So, even though he's keeping his eyes and ears open, he's off the case."

"How do you feel about that?" Annabelle asked

"I'm just trying to move on and let God take care of it," Leslie said as they checked out at the front counter. "I do wish Ryan had never gotten caught up in it. But I think even he has moved on. He hasn't talked about it lately, so that is good."

"Well, I think we have everything, including the King Cake baby. I just can't believe he will go to school soon. He was just a baby last week, and now he's a big boy."

"I know. Don't remind me. I can't stand the thought of him being away at school," Leslie said with tears coming to her eyes.

"He'll be fine, wait and see. He'll love it. He's such a talented little boy, full of curiosity and the desire to learn. It's you I'm worried about," Annabelle said giving Leslie a little side hug before hailing a taxi for their ride home.

Chapter **31**

Nick wasn't sure why he was so angry, he just knew he didn't like thinking about Mama and the things she told him. It was thirty or more years in his past. He had almost forgotten about the pretty young thing he left with Mama and now he was dealing with more information than he wanted to know. According to Mama the private detective's wife didn't know who he was or at least not yet anyway. Now it seemed Mama was determined to interfere in his life. *Why tell her now? What good would come of them knowing?* He shook his head as he drove past the house wondering if the mother of his daughter still lived there. *Did she get married and raise her daughter with other children?* he thought, parked across from the house where she had lived. He remembered when he met Leslie at the Bordeaux House he thought he knew her from somewhere. Little did he know she was his daughter?

She was right under his nose the whole time. His buddies were building the studio in the back of her house. *Why did Mama see the resemblance and he didn't?* Because it was a onetime thing. A very wrong thing. One that haunted him through the years especially after Mama's lecture that night when he came back to get the girl he left behind. Back then he wanted to set things right. But he didn't get the chance, so he moved on and finally put it behind him. Sitting across the street, he watched the people coming and going but didn't recognize anyone. He had to figure out some way to see his daughter without her knowing. Then there was her husband, the private detective. He would have to be extremely careful.

"Hey mister, are you lost?" a young boy said through the open passenger window.

"No. But thanks anyway."

"So, what are you doing sitting here," the boy asked.

None of your business kid. He thought but said, "I'm resting before I hit the road again. I don't want to fall asleep driving," he said trying to keep his attitude in check.

"Oh. Well, have a nice day."

"Yeah."

Turning the key in the ignition, he took one last look, then he headed out of town toward the highway. He wondered if there was an APB out on his truck. A.J. was back home. And, unless she were pressing charges, there would be no reason to be looking for him. Since he had treated her with respect and sent her home on the bus, he was sure she wasn't going to say anything. Just to be safe, he would take the back roads back to New Orleans. First stop, the paint shop. Everyone knew the big red monster of a truck, so he had to change the color. Second stop, the barber. It was time to lose the curly locks and beard. A new wardrobe was in order too. The only thing still apparent to anyone who knew him was his attitude, his ego. Maybe Mercy was right. A little religion wouldn't hurt.

So far, his plan was working out. His truck was now a shiny black, his locks tamed, and new clothes made him presentable. As he looked in the mirror, he hardly recognized the handsome 'ole guy staring back at him. He had seen a small church coming into New Orleans parish, and since it was out a ways he didn't think he would know anyone.

Sunday came, and he drove up to the church and parked. Not many cars were in the parking lot. *Maybe this isn't such a good idea*, he thought. He didn't want to stand out among people who knew each other. He backed out of the parking place and headed back into the French Quarter. He wasn't Catholic, so St. Louis Cathedral was out of the question. He drove around for a while then uptown he came to another church. Again, he parked and then went inside. The service was well under way when he found a seat at the back. The Choir had just finished singing, and the pastor stood to give his message.

Being uncomfortable in this foreign atmosphere, he tried to listen to the message but found he couldn't concentrate on what the man was saying. *What is he talking about?* Nick asked himself. *God is my salvation? So, why do I need God's salvation?* Nick was confused, and he felt ignorant. He didn't remember learning this in Sunday school as a young boy. But back then he wasn't trying to learn anything. The more he listened to the pastor the more sense it was making. Maybe there was something to this God thing. He remembered singing "Jesus loves me" but now he was learning why Jesus loved him.

A couple of Sundays passed, and each message was making more sense. He finally waited until the service was over and asked the pastor to answer a few questions. After his talk with the pastor, he was sure he had the whole idea of the Trinity, God, Son, and Holy Spirit down. Curiosity prompted a trip to the bookstore where he bought a Bible. *What's going on with you Nick 'ole boy, this God thing? Do you think you can really pull this off? Maybe with strangers like some people at church, but what about people that know you? Will they see through this charade?* His thoughts swirled around in his head trying to make sense of his actions. *"Really, a Bible?"* he said out loud carrying the sack containing the Bible to the truck. Sitting in the truck with the motor running, he opened the Bible and there in Psalms 51.1 *Have mercy on me, O God, according to your unfailing love;* he continued to read, he couldn't stop reading. *If all I have to do is repent and ask God's forgiveness like Mercy said....*

Not being much of a reader, Nick surprised himself at not being able to put this book down. Every chance he got he would open to different places in this Bible and find it applied to him. It was as if this God really knew him. Not only that, but there were answers to the situations Nick found himself in. It was fascinating, and he kept reading looking for some way to dispel the teachings. Not ready to accept the ideas presented but anxious to read the next chapter, he was becoming aware of a profound change taking place in his being. *Maybe this is why Mama and Mercy love this God so much. And this Jesus... wow, how can anyone be that perfect and strong?* Of course, he knew about Jesus and the cross, he wasn't born under a rock, or at least he didn't think he was. But, now he was learning things about this Jesus that caused him to get emotional thinking about how He suffered such pain and humiliation hanging on that cross, so sinners like himself, could be forgiven and have eternal life. Definitely a new point of view for him.

Since he and his partner had parted ways, his income had dwindled, and it wouldn't be long before he would have to figure out a way to make money, preferably within the law. Not wanting to expose himself to the construction business in case he ran across someone he knew, he started looking at the want ads for anything that fit his circumstances. One day there was an ad that made him laugh, but then he thought, *Why not?*

Chapter **32**

Everyone, including Ryan, was busy getting ready for the big day. Rented table and chairs filled the area near where the bounce house would be. Sydney was using helium to blow up the balloons with Ryan close by helping to put the balloons in a big net bag.

"This is fun, Dad," Ryan said stuffing another balloon in the bag.

"Careful, don't let the other balloons out of the bag," Sidney said laughing at Ryan trying to push the helium-filled balloons in the big net bag. "We're almost finished. A couple more and the bag will be full."

"When will my friends be here, Dad?"

"Later this afternoon, Son. We have a lot of things to do before they come. Are you getting excited?"

"Yes!" he said loud and clear.

Meanwhile, in the house, Leslie, Annabelle, and Daisy were busy making refreshments. Leslie was making the King Cake with the plastic baby inside, Daisy was making fresh lemonade, and Annabelle was putting goodies in little individual bags and tying pieces of ribbon around the top.

"How are you doing over there?" Leslie asked Annabelle.

"Do you think we got enough of these little bags?"

"I got thirty. That's how many invitations I sent out. What do you think?"

"That's probably more than enough, since some of them may not be able to come."

"That's true, so I think we're okay," Leslie said putting the cake in the oven.

Daisy put the gallon jugs of lemonade in the refrigerator and told Leslie she was going outside to help put plastic on the tables. About that time the truck carrying the bounce house was backing down the driveway in back of the house toward the side yard.

Ryan was jumping up and down with excitement as the truck came to a stop. The men got out, and after Sidney showed them where he wanted it to go, they began to unload everything. Ryan watched wide-eyed as they began to blow up the bounce house. As each section was filled with air, Ryan yelled and clapped. When it was ready, they asked Ryan if he wanted to test it. Ryan ran and climbed into the bounce house and started jumping up and down.

"Come on Dad, this is fun."

"I better not Ryan, this is for you kids."

"It's alright, sir. You can do it too," one of the men told him.

So, Sidney jumped in beside Ryan with both of them yelling. Just then they sat up and saw Leslie standing at the entry wiping her hands on her apron.

"I see you boys are already having fun," she said smiling at them.

Sidney got up and came out leaving Ryan to play a little bit longer. He took Leslie's arm and guided her away from earshot of Ryan.

"I couldn't get a clown, but I managed to get a mime. I think that will work well along with the King Cake theme don't you think?"

"I think it's perfect. After all, we're in New Orleans. Good job Sid," she said giving him a kiss on the cheek.

"Well, thank you, my lady," Sidney said giving her a hug.

Leslie was thankful that A.J. and her kids volunteered to help with keeping order at the party. With thirty kids and not many parents staying they needed all the adult help they could get. They set up different stations for refreshments. One table for drinks. One table for prizes and dress up items such as masks and fake hair and hats. Last but not least was a table for the King Cake. Different colors covered each table, the plastic taped down so the wind wouldn't catch it and take off with it.

Everything in place, they all went into the kitchen and fixed a plate of food for their lunch. Afterward, Ryan was told to go to his room to rest.

"Mom, I'm five now. I don't need a nap," Ryan protested.

"Ryan. Do as your mother says," Sidney said firmly.

After Ryan went to his room, they got out his present and wrapped it.

"I don't know about you, but I could use a nap myself," Leslie said.

"Let's do it."

Daisy and Annabelle had gone home to get changed, and she and Jeffrey would pick up Jonathon on their way back. It would be good to have Jeffrey and Jonathon at the party to help with the chaos too.

Chapter *33*

Nick stood in the dressing room looking in the full-length mirror. *Was this a coincidence? Or like Mercy called it, a God thing.* Whatever it was he was grateful. He began to practice the moves. He had seen people on the street in front of the cathedral and on the church steps doing this, and it didn't seem all that hard, but now he appreciated their skill. After a while, he thought he was ready to put on the makeup and outfit he could hide behind, while seeing not only his daughter but his grandson without detection.

He shaved his face close to the skin then applied baby oil to make the white pigment go on smoother. Soon his face was covered even his lips and eyelids.

"If I didn't know it was me I wouldn't be able to recognize this 'ole man," Nick said leaning forward to touch up some spots where the skin was showing before shaking powder all over his face causing him to sneeze several times.

"That looks really good for your first time," the clown sitting next to him said.

"Thank you for your help," Nick said. "I appreciate it."

He reached for the hangers holding a white long puffy sleeve blouse and black tights. The long sleeves were perfect because they covered the tattoos up and down his arms. He felt weird in the tights. It was like wearing a wetsuit. That, he remembered well, while working on the ship and having to go into the water to repair pipes in the engine room when they ruptured. Those times were far behind him. *Now, look at me,* he thought, a performer of a different kind. Ready to go, he put on the final touches, white gloves and long black hair tied on with a scarf.

"You might want to wait on the gloves unless your steering wheel is spotlessly clean if you know what I mean?" the clown advised.

"Good idea. Thanks again."

One last look and he went to his truck. He didn't need the directions given to him by the owner of the clown business, he knew exactly how to get there. Parking off the street he sat a while getting up his nerve. He wouldn't have to talk, so his voice wouldn't give him away. The whole thing was almost too perfect. *Well, here we go ready or not.* He thought, putting on the gloves. Grabbing the case full of Mardi Gras beads he got out of the truck.

The party was in full swing with kids everywhere. He took a deep breath and looked around the area. His eyes landed on a beautiful woman in a long skirt, sleeveless blouse and a large wide brim hat. Standing next to her was another attractive woman with long hair draped over her shoulder, little makeup, in a long yellow dress with a halter top. *Is that A.J.? What if she recognizes me? But, how could she?* His nerves were ramping up, and he was almost ready to leave when Sidney approached him.

"Come on in. We will get the kids settled down with refreshments while you perform," he said leading the way.

Nick put his case full of beads on the ground in front of him and waited for everyone to sit down at their tables with their piece of King Cake.

"Okay, everyone listen. Before you eat your King Cake, remember the one that gets a plastic baby inside wins a prize. So, while you eat we have a mime that will perform for you."

Nick opened the case of beads and began to mime as he took some beads and put them around each child's neck. He would go back to the case, and to the delight of his audience, he would put more beads around their necks.

Suddenly he realized that Ryan was choking. With everyone shouting and jumping up and down, he was the only one that noticed. He threw the beads down and shouted, "Leslie!"

He picked Ryan up and started lifting Ryan's chest to dislodge whatever was choking him. He tried again, and suddenly the plastic came out along with a stream of blood.

"Call an ambulance," he shouted.

Sidney and Leslie ran to Ryan. Sidney took him from Nick and ran toward his car that was blocked by Nick's truck.

"Here, take my truck or let me drive while you hold him," Nick said opening the door so Sidney and Leslie could get in.

He backed out into the street and turned on his hazard lights, then headed for the emergency room. They passed by the fire station, and Nick saw the emergency response unit inside and pulled into the drive with his horn blaring. He jumped out of the truck and ran inside. The paramedics came out and took Ryan into the ambulance. Leslie stayed with Ryan and Sidney jumped in the front seat of Nick's truck as he pulled out behind the ambulance.

"I can't thank you enough for what you did back there, not only dislodging that plastic thing but having the forethought to stop at the fire station," Sidney said.

"He's going to be alright," Nick said not only to reassure Sidney but himself.

They arrived at the emergency room, and Sidney got out of the truck and went to the back of the ambulance. Nick parked his truck and he went inside. After examining Ryan, they told Leslie and Sidney that Ryan would need surgery to close the tear in his throat to stop the bleeding.

Nick stood off to the side and watched Leslie and Sidney hug each other. Leslie was crying, and Sidney was trying to keep her calm. Nick walked over to them.

"Maybe…we should pray," he said hesitantly. *"God be with our little boy. Take good care of him for us. Thank you…."* Then he remembered, *"Oh, in Jesus' Name. Amen."*

Leslie turned around. She knew. Nick looked at her with tears running down his face smearing his white makeup.

"You saved your grandson's life…"

ANOTHER BEGINNING

EPILOGUE

In the days following Ryan's surgery, Nick would put on the mime outfit and entertain him while he convalesced at home. Ryan watched Nick's mimes and since he wasn't supposed to talk he and Nick would communicate with hand jesters. Leslie watched this interaction between Nick and Ryan every day. She began to see a new Nick, and as the days went by, she began to realize the hand God had in all that had happened. Then one day she heard Ryan speak for the first time.

"Thank you for being my friend."

"You're welcome, Ryan. I like being friends with you."

"Can't you see God's plan in all of this Sidney?" she told him one evening. "I think it may be time to introduce Ryan to his grandfather.

"There may be a problem here," Sidney said. "Remember the picture of Nick that Ryan saw? He was terrified of that Nick. How are we going to explain that?"

They decided to invite Nick over in his mime outfit, so Ryan would be comfortable while the three of them explained everything to him. Nick knew the time would come when he would have to face the music so to speak, and it had never bothered him as much as it did now. He didn't want his grandson to know he was a thief.

Nick arrived at the Rye home early so he could talk to Leslie. Ryan was upstairs, and Leslie was in the kitchen. Sidney let Nick in, and after being told he wanted to talk to Leslie before seeing Ryan, Sidney went upstairs to keep Ryan occupied.

"Leslie, before we go any further, I want to apologize for everything I have done to cause you any pain. I'm pretty sure Mama told you everything. I was young, I know that is no excuse, but I made a big mistake that I have regretted ever since. I never knew about you until very recently and was surprised by the fact you're a wonderful wife and mother. I suspect your mother is very proud of you and the job she did raising you."

"Nick before you go any further I need to tell you something. My mother never married. She raised me herself until I was eight years old when she died of pneumonia. My aunt, her sister, raised me in a Christian home with my cousins. Now all of that said. I was furious and shocked when Mama told me about you. I struggled with the truth for many weeks. Ryan is the light of my life as I was the light of my mother's life and she chose not to tell me about you. However, as a Christian, I know Jesus died on the cross for our sins. I'm aware that you have changed, and I forgive you but now we need to protect Ryan from any fears he may have about you."

"What do you mean?"

Leslie told Nick that Sidney had been looking for him in connection to a jewelry theft and had a sketch of him that Ryan saw. She also told him about Ryan seeing him when he came to give his friends a ride.

Nick shook his head. "What if he's afraid of me?"

"Nick, all of this, is in God's hands. Don't you see His hand in all of this?"

"Yes, I do."

About that time, Sidney and Ryan came downstairs. Ryan ran to Nick and put his arms around him.

"Hi Nick, are you going to stay for dinner?"

"We'll see Ryan," Nick said.

"Please mom, can Nick stay for dinner."

"Let's go to the table, we want to tell you something," Leslie said putting her hand on his shoulder to lead him to the table.

They all sat down, then Leslie told Ryan that the person he knew as Nick was also his grandfather. Ryan didn't hesitate to yell, "Yeah!" The thought that his friend was also his grandfather excited him. Then curiosity set in and the questions began in typical Ryan style.

"Does he know?" Ryan said looking at Nick.

"Know what, Ryan?" Leslie said.

"That he's my grandfather?" Ryan said confused.

"Yes."

"But where has he been?"

"What do you mean?" Leslie said.

"You know, Mom, before he was my friend?"

"That is what we want to talk to you about." Sidney said as he pulled out the sketch he had made of Nick, the one Ryan had seen.

"Ryan do you remember this picture."

"Dad, that's the picture of the bad guy."

Nick swallowed hard. It hurt to hear those words coming from this little boy, his grandson. He tried to keep his composure.

"Ryan, remember in Sunday School when we learned why Jesus died on the cross," Leslie said.

"So, if we do something bad God will forgive us," he said with pride that he knew the answer.

"So, if someone you know does something bad do you think that because God can forgive them, you should also forgive that person?" Leslie said watching for his reaction.

"But Mom, when I do bad things you send me to my room."

"That's true. God forgives us, and we forgive each other, but sometimes we are still punished for doing something bad. Can you understand what I'm saying?" Leslie asked hopefully.

"I think so."

"So, son, the man in this picture did something bad. He took things that weren't his. And now he will be punished and go to jail for a while."

"But we will forgive him?" Ryan queried.

"Yes," Leslie said.

It was time to reveal Nick's true identity. Nick prepared for the worst as Sidney explained that Nick was the man in the picture. But not to be afraid because he was also his friend. Then Leslie reminded Ryan that Nick was his grandfather as Nick went to remove the makeup. When he returned, he looked at Ryan.

"Are you still my friend?" Ryan said.

"Always, Ryan. And while I'm in jail, I'll write you letters, and you can show me all the things you're learning in school. Is that a deal?"

"I forgive you, Nick," Ryan said with tears.

"Thank you, Ryan. I love you very much, and I'm so happy God put us together," Nick said hugging Ryan.

"I love you grandfather."

www.ingramcontent.com/pod-product-compliance
Lightning Source LLC
Chambersburg PA
CBHW021151110726
47900CB00002B/520